THE 1MAG1NAT1ON
OF THE STATE

Redacted Stories

Alex M. Pruteanu

THE

IMAGINATION

OF

THE STATE

Redacted Stories

Alex M. Pruteanu

Alex M. Pruteanu
www.swine.wordpress.com

Editors: Teresa Chapman & Brian Carter Gaj
Layout: Teresa Chapman
Cover Design: Margaret Burgan
Cover Image: Cassandra Lynne
Author Photo: Teresa Chapman

Published by Independent Talent Group, Inc.
Fairlawn, OH 44333

ISBN-13: 978-0-9840093-4-3

Printed in the United States of America

CONTENTS

CONTENTS

MY FBI FILE

THE FOLLOWING INFORMATION was released to me in 2003 after a pending (three years), protracted formal request to FBI headquarters, under the U.S. State Department's Freedom of Information Act (FOIA):

██████████, Installation Services Division, United States Postal Service (USPS) Management Academy, 250 Khartoum St. Potomac, MD, advised that on January 28, 1993, he learned from a confidential source that Alex M. Pruteanu (AMP), a file clerk with employee number 20687N5, was allegedly writing obscene and politically seditious articles for the City Paper (weekly) magazine of Washington D.C. and that he was not married to the individual listed as the beneficiary for his Life and Health Benefits Insurance.

██████████ advised that he reviewed AMP's official personnel file and noted that he listed one ██████ ██████

1

of 5526 Good Luck Road, Lanham, MD, as his wife on Standard Form 53, Designation of Beneficiary, Federal Employee Group Life Insurance Act of 1954, and on Standard Form 1772 Designation of Beneficiary Unpaid Compensation of Deceased Civilian Employee, both dated November 1, 1992.

███████████ advised that on February 20, 1993 between approximately 10:00 p.m. and 11:00 p.m. he interviewed AMP at the terminal annex, USPS, Kensington, MD. During this interview, AMP acknowledged having written twenty-four articles for the weekly, independent magazine City Paper, in a series titled "(S)WINE—FICTION...SOMETIMES." Use of parentheses around the "S" is intentional, not a typo. For the official record: it's a play on words meant to be humorous. He stated that these articles have appeared in two dozen issues of the City Paper and that he is paid by its editorial board for these articles. Sometimes payment is delivered in the form of bottles of whisky. He explained that his articles are "an inter-mixture of fiction and fact" and are "highly romanticized in order to give the story juice and muscle." He further elaborated that he writes these articles "for sheer joy and relief of stress brought on by various elements in daily, modern life . . ." He acknowledged being the author of such articles titled "Gillette to Consumers: The Hell with Everything, We're Doing Five Blades" and "The Journal of the American Medical Association: 4 Out of 5 Doctors Think the 5th is an Idiot."

███████████ further advised that AMP admitted to him that he entered into a common-law marriage several years ago with ███████████ who calls herself ███████████. AMP claimed that ███████████ does not want marriage and that ███████████ ███████████ better off with this arrangement. He stated that this ███████████ and lives, "I don't know, someplace in the Midwest like Missoula or Terre

Haute." ████████████ ████████ Ms. ████████ admitted
that she shares AMP's apartment and bed on occasion for limited
periods of a few days at a time. She also complained that AMP is
quite an inconsiderate dweller and leaves the toilet seat up
when she's there. She believes he does this on purpose and only
when she is in residence.

████████, Installation Services Division stated that AMP
has an extremely poor employment record, fraught with scores
of bad reviews because of excessive absenteeism. He stated
according to his record, AMP uses "ill health" as a reason for
being absent.

████████ stated that he knows nothing at all concerning
AMP's associates (and that it's highly likely that AMP indeed
has no associates at all), reputation, or loyalty to the United
States, despite being a (pseudo) federal employee who has
agreed to an official oath (required of every federal employee,
pseudo or otherwise). He stated, however, that based upon AMP's
admitted authorship of the above-mentioned articles in the
City Paper and the fact that he is living in a common-law
marriage, he would say that AMP's moral character leaves much
to be desired. He stated for this reason, he would not recommend
AMP for retention as an employee of the USPS.

On March 23, 1993 ████████ of New Carrollton, MD, advised
████████, Installation Services Division that his title is
████████████████ of the apartments at 5234 Crescent Green,
College Park, MD. He stated that AMP has resided in the
apartment at 5234 Crescent Green for the past three years. He
stated he couldn't give the exact date that AMP moved to that
address, as he has no records of his tenancy. A large portion of
the apartment complex's files perished in a suspicious fire
started in the storage room located in the basement of the main
office.

He stated that AMP is an excellent tenant who never associates with any of his neighbors. He stated that AMP keeps to himself while in residence and never seems to have any visitors. ███████, however, stated that there is an enormous, sometimes egregious, amount of garbage being generated by AMP, all in the form of empty gin bottles, which AMP has a tendency to leave by the door, outside his unit in several large cardboard boxes for many days at a time before he physically hauls (in a truck) the refuse to the designated receptacles on the premises of the property. ████████ further stated that since the garbage mainly consists of empty bottles, there is no offensive odor emanating, and small animals such as mice, rats, cats, opossums, armadillos, sloths (??), mole rats (?), and alamiquis (???), are not usually attracted to AMP's refuse "unless they're drunkard" (humorous attempt duly noted in quotation marks by interviewer). ███████ proceeded to laugh heartily after that comment for quite a long time, making the situation at first uncomfortable, and then unbearably annoying for the interviewer. At times, █████████ admitted he has removed several dozen empty bottles from AMP's pile by the door and returned them to the liquor store in order to redeem deposit fees which, according to ██████, sometimes reach as high as fifteen dollars. ████████ further stated that as far as he knows, AMP is not married and attested that he has never seen any women in or around his apartment. In fact, he has never seen anyone other than AMP in residence. He stated that he feels that he does not know AMP well enough to comment on his character, associates, reputation, or loyalty to the United States, and stated that he could neither offer nor decline any recommendation of his (AMP's) character for that reason. Note: ███████ inquired about some type of payment in exchange for his testimony. The interviewer explained that this is an official investigation into AMP's record as a USPS employee and that no such recompense was forthcoming. But after a considerable amount of time bargaining for a remuneratory solution, the interviewer agreed to buy ▓▓▓▓▓▓ a meal at Shakey's All You Can Eat Buffet in Hyattsville, MD.

On September 13, 1993, AMP made an official statement with the USPS's Office of Complaints and Grievances ▓▓▓▓▓▓

▓▓

▓▓

▓▓

▓▓

▓▓

▓▓

▓▓

▓▓▓▓▓▓▓▓▓▓▓▓▓▓▓▓ opening act consisted of a juggler who performed his feats with various sharp objects such as a machete, ▓▓▓▓▓▓, a medieval mace, and a sickle. ▓▓▓▓▓▓

▓▓

▓▓▓▓▓▓▓▓▓▓▓▓▓▓▓▓▓▓▓▓▓▓ rated the performance highly unsatisfactory, especially the quality of the sound of the drum set. ▓▓▓▓▓▓▓▓▓▓▓▓▓▓▓▓▓▓▓▓▓▓▓▓▓▓▓▓▓▓

▓▓

▓▓▓▓▓▓▓▓▓▓▓▓▓▓▓▓▓▓▓▓▓▓▓▓▓▓▓▓▓▓ Currently, AMP is in litigation with ▓▓▓▓▓▓▓▓▓, the company that sold him the tickets to the performance.

Recommendation for AMP's employment with the USPS is termination with no additional benefits or severance.

▓▓

▓▓

▓▓▓▓▓▓ or, given the potential for aggressive behavior, the move could be justified as a "reduction in force." If that course of action is chosen, a going-away party could be arranged at a very low cost; anticipated attendance is between one and three other willing co-workers. Budget can come in under $100, reserved for: one cold cuts platter, paper plates/cups, two large bottles of soda, and a black ballpoint pen (Uniball by Signo) given as a parting token of appreciation for AMP's years of service with the USPS. Also available is a small, stuffed replica of a postman (cloth with cotton stuffing, made in China, retail: $5.99).

Report prepared and filed by: ███████, Installation Services Division, United States Postal Service Management Academy. Office hours: between ██████████████████ ██████, emergency assistance available 24 hours, not all in a row. ██ ████████████████████████████████ Plasticine and mercury.

EVERYTHING RHYMES WITH ORANGE

(Published in The Prague Revue, 2014)

EVERY ONE OF US at the orphanage knew that Saint Paul wasn't going to make the long haul, which was a glib assertion given his track record and the number of birthdays he'd ticked off in this godforsaken place already. Plus, he was of Russian and German descent, and that alone should have shut us up right quick. Those people live forever and through everything. Many of us were two and three years younger than he; we were new to the world, dumb, and we held dearly to our prediction (or hope).

"Come winter we'll bury him with the others next to the outhouse, you'll see; he's feeble."

"With what? They won't give us shovels."

"We'll have to dig the frozen earth with our hands if we need to. You'll see. He's a goner."

"Keep the soup spoons one day and we could all use those to—"

"Eh, soup spoons, they count those, you sap."

"He won't go without first spreading tuberculosis to all of us, the donkey."

"Or whooping cough."

"The goddamned donkey."

We canonized Saint Paul one summer evening while we were out in the yard scrubbing the legs of our metal bunks clean of bed bugs. There was something satisfying about taking a wire brush to the metal, squashing the parasites, and seeing streaks of blood magically appear and ooze down slowly to the barren, moist earth covering the yard, despite the sickening implications. The beds were bleeding, all of them. What a sight. The bugs were always back, but those few nights sleeping free of infestation made up for anything and everything that eventually came. And some kind of new hardship always did.

We made him a saint for the same reason that we wished him dead: a private, morally conflicting love-hate relationship with his longevity and fortitude in the face of his ailment. Anyone hanging on to life like him for so long must surely be blessed. Our prediction of his quick demise (or, rather, our wish) was rooted in our own fears; it was a way of metaphorically pushing him to the front of the line before our own turns came. We were old enough, then, to fear death, despite our belief in God.

But Saint Paul didn't. He didn't fear death, and he didn't believe in anything mystical. He couldn't have. He could barely wipe his own ass without falling into the outhouse hole. It was because of this presumed lack of faith we assigned to him that we felt good about wishing him dead. And maybe it was also because of it that we canonized him. It was our sarcastic dig at an accidental sinner. What better way than to make him a saint? And the miracle required for such a burden? The miracle was that Saint Paul was still alive.

He first came to us in the middle of a ruthless autumn, a year fraught with famine, lice, and wind. The director of the orphanage literally kicked Saint Paul in the small of his back as he deposited him into our dormitory, nearly breaking his spine.

"Two to a bunk, you horse's ass," the director said after the ruthless strike. "You understand anything?"

All Saint Paul did was scratch at his bad leg.

Our first thought, as we stared at this crippled, feral cat standing in the middle of the stench-filled room, was: another mouth to feed. Which meant: an extra gram or maybe even two sliced off our already anemic daily chunk of bread. Another bloody mouth to feed. And all Saint Paul did was scratch at his lame leg, not ever understanding what a tremendous burden he had just become to us.

"What's wrong with you, Quasimodo?" someone yelled from the back of the dormitory.

"He's deaf and dumb. Ate his own tongue with mustard and horseradish."

The entire room roared as Saint Paul dragged his crippled leg behind, right shoulder pointing up. Later, in our stupidity and mysticism, we grew to believe that his deformed shoulder joint singled out the actions and existence of God—always pointing at the heavens, as if to say, "He's judging you." And that interpretation transformed into disbelief, envy, and animosity for all of us. How could this thin, pale feral boy with a gammy leg and a crooked shoulder define dominion over the wretched life in an orphanage? How could this thick-headed gimp believe in Our Father? It was impossible.

Saint Paul.

Once, when we were starving so badly we felt our insides fusing together in excruciating union, Saint Paul's leg, dragging behind near the base of a tree, miraculously dug up what we at first thought were just some ordinary black roots. Later, I would learn that only the most sophisticated noses of dogs or pigs would detect such culinary treasure, and people in restaurants all over the world would pay heavy money for a taste.

"These ain't no roots, comrades . . . the gimp just dug up some kind of mushrooms!"

We ate them raw and dirty with the soft streaks of earth from which they were plucked by a kid's lucky bum leg. They looked like pieces of coal, but they filled the aching spaces in our bellies, and that night the entire boys' dormitory slept soundly, undisturbed by moaning intestines.

This kind of dumb, timely chance coupled with Saint Paul's indifference to hardship in general (he seemed to smile all the time, although Adrian said it was a facial tick or a muscle frozen stiff—God only knows with these stunted people) only exacerbated our envy and longing for his demise. We concluded that he couldn't tell whether he was dead or alive, hungry or full, and so he continued to be a burden on our measly food rations. If only he would go away—poof—we'd get back our requisite gram or two of bread.

Saint Paul.

He drew the most incredible, vivid scenes into the ankle-deep snow, using a twig or a stick. Often, we'd see him squatting in the yard crafting his tableaus long after we'd gone back inside, shivering and shriveling from the cold. The orphanage workers didn't care to bring him in. They didn't care about any of us. It was a place for us to wait out death. For them, as well.

"Honestly, I wouldn't give a bit of a damn if he just bought it right there," said Adrian.

"He's too thick to realize anything; he'll forget . . . I say let him freeze. Why should any of us go out there and bring him back? He's as old as us; old enough to take responsibility."

"Older."

"He can come in by himself."

"He's a thick, is what he is."

"A frozen thick."

The picture that I loved the most, the one that Saint Paul drew often into the snow, was a scene dominated by thick, poofy swirls floating randomly above a village. For years after, often coming back to that magical world etched into the icy snow by this lame boy, I mistakenly thought the swirls were cotton candy—what else was the mind of a crippled, deaf, and dumb kid capable of creating? Thick swabs of cotton candy in the sky only made sense. But it wasn't cotton candy at all.

The art album in which I saw Saint Paul's snow picture decades later and a hemisphere removed from the orphanage, was resting on a friend's coffee table in his small flat. It was a large, hard cover, thick collection of Van Gogh's complete works, and I picked it up on chance, looking to kill time before some forgettable social event at which we were expected that evening. Saint Paul's picture was called "The Starry Night," and depicted the view from Van Gogh's asylum room in Saint-Rémy-de-Provence, in 1889. That's what the caption underneath the remarkable scenery indicated. That's where Saint Paul took us nearly every snowy day during that time in our childhoods; only we were too envious, too narrow-minded, and too ill-cultured to understand.

Kitchen duty consisted of peeling potatoes. Hundreds and hundreds of potatoes that were to be made into soup or mashed or baked (we imagined) and that none of us boys at the orphanage ever saw after they were peeled and stored in gigantic, steaming buckets. Gigi said they probably fed the administrators and their families, the Haves. The Have Nots peeled potatoes and thought with anger and jealousy about what the Haves had.

"They probably hoard away chunks of chocolate, too."

With the small paring knife, I would start at the top of the elliptical tuber and, daydreaming of Saint Paul's swirling clouds of cotton candy, winding in a gradually widening curve, I would shave off the brown, earthy skin until it fell helplessly in one flexible piece onto the floor.

Saint Paul's various skin ailments, fevers, and horrific coughs (always bringing up bloody, sticky phlegm) often excused him from kitchen duty, especially in the cold months. We became increasingly more enraged at his fortunate confinement to his bunk while we spent hours peeling potatoes, cursing and spitting and thinking up scenarios of torture and revenge.

"The bloody cripple. He's laughing at all of us working dogs, with his goddamned shivers and fevers and whatever in hell else he's got."

We finally convinced ourselves that to share our minuscule ration of daily gruel with a non-thinking cripple whose maladies constantly got him out of any work, particularly kitchen duty, was a severely punishable quid pro quo to be carried out by each of us. Saint Paul, it seemed, was never going to die from anything: not cold, not blood-tainted coughs, not crippling fever.

Adrian's plan made the most sense and gave us all a chance at revenge against Saint Paul, so we swore to it on a makeshift Bible. At the end of kitchen duty, we each smuggled out a clandestine potato—not too big to be suspicious, but fat enough that it would do the job properly. We hid it down our pants, in the front, so the bulge wouldn't look suspect to the administrators. Once in the dormitory, we dropped the tuber surreptitiously into one of our socks, and thus we had our weapon.

That night, as he slept, we aimed to pay back Saint Paul for his indolence or handicap or . . . saintliness. I felt sick to my stomach with hunger and guilt. All I could think about was eating the raw potato that now lived in my sock. If I did that, then I wouldn't have to take my revenge on Saint Paul. But, like everyone else, I was sworn to the plan. And probably like everyone else, I went along with it because I convinced myself that a gimp wouldn't realize what was happening to him anyway. Or because the others were doing it and so must I.

As we each took a swing with our potatoes safely held in our knotted-up socks (only one hit per boy, that was the plan), Saint Paul's ribcage began to crack under the blows. Some of us hit the legs, others the stomach. The head was off limits. That was the plan. One by one we got in our blows quickly, before retreating to our bunks in silence. I don't know if the others felt the guilt inside the guts like I did. Some I could tell didn't; they were the ones winding up like a windmill and swinging at Saint Paul as hard as they could, snickering or smiling. They were ruthless. We all were flawed and inadequate in our own way. It's what the orphanage had taught us best.

Some boys aimed and swung but didn't look, as if not witnessing their own violent act somehow exculpated them; as if by not looking they could detach themselves from their own bodies and actions and minds. I was one of those. And at the very last moment, I held up on my blow, hoping not to hurt the lame boy too badly. On my way back to my bunk, Adrian, who had seen my hesitation, shook his head with disgust and whispered, "Coward."

In the middle of the weird, silent mayhem, as he lay on his back suffering thirty-odd blows from freshly peeled potatoes tied up in dirty socks and launched at his fragile body by ruthless, depraved creatures who knew nothing but violence and hunger, Saint Paul opened his eyes and looked toward the window. He did not know the meaning of, nor would he ever understand forgiveness or godliness, or sainthood; no one had ever spoken to him about virtue, suffering, or sacrifice. The horrid beating he endured was merely part of the world that night. He didn't feel about it any more or less than what it simply meant.

But at the window, outside in the frigid, dimly lit yard that held a thick layer of icy, thigh-deep snow, Saint Paul saw the silhouetted torso of his father. It was his father before he became his father: a young man, dressed in officer's uniform, the shape of the epaulets clearly visible, delineating each shoulder in that particular military way which only epaulets can. Cradling in his arms, like a precious infant, the officer held three oranges. Saint Paul knew they were oranges. He smelled them. He tasted the slightly bitter pith, and tart, almost blood-red carpels. He knew they came from the other part of the world, way down below the equator: Maseru, Bloemfontein, Pretoria.

The best navel oranges came from South Africa, and that's what Saint Paul's father had brought to him that night as he lay on his back, his bones shattering under the strikes of angry, peeled fists that once grew in the soil.

MA, IN FRAGMENTS
(Published in The Doctor T. J. Eckleburg Review, 2013)

THE FACTORY ACROSS the river blows third shift over. When she opens her eyes it's a quarter to five. She shifts slowly and props herself up on her good side and looks at the small clock ticking loudly on the nightstand beside her bed, next to the icon of Jesus offering mercy. It says five-thirty. *Clack-clack-clack*, the second hand sounds like an axe splitting wood, and she strains to look through the window at the dark yard now peppered with shadows of proud hens announcing the arrival of their eggs. Little, bragging dinosaurs strutting comically about.

★

The room is cold. The wind shoulders hard against the windows and the glass makes loud, cracking noises like old redwoods bending in a gale. She reaches for her glasses and tries to push up a little higher against the headboard.

Should I make the fire, Ma?

Be a good boy will you, she says.

And the tea?

And the tea, she says. Do it like your father, she crosses herself. Make it in the metal mug. Hot. Steaming so.

Ma, it'll take the enamel off your teeth. The doctor said . . .

Be a good boy will you now.

Should I cut some bacon?

Not today. I'm not hungry.

Ma, if you don't eat first thing . . .

Not today, she says again and pats down her permed, gray hair on the side. And then she remembers in a controlled panic: The *parastas* for your father is this afternoon.

The wind reminds her with a quick, heavy gust that it's late autumn and the rainy season is making threats against the outdoor wake.

Will you split some wood later? Nicoletta is bringing stuffed cabbage leaves and sausage. I made mushrooms and garlic and a pot of borscht and head cheese. Someone is bringing wine. Dimi? Did you hear about the wood?

★

She lifts up on her elbow to focus instead on a grinning, naked toddler sitting in a wooden tub in front of the bed, in hot water among soaking laundry.

Jesus, she says. She flings her head toward the window and yells: Come get your drawers out of the tub, man. They've been soaking all day.

She can't see him, just his pitchfork rising and lowering behind the fence, disheveled and disintegrating little piles of hay being thrown into the barn.

You hear me? She bangs with her fist on the wall, beneath the window. Come and get your pants, deaf old fool! Dimi, get out of that dirty water, boy.

She looks at the clock again and realizes that she's set it forty-five minutes ahead.

She's always done that.

★

Go down and get your father, she says. Go before he drinks his entire wages down there, the bum . . . Stop fidgeting and go already, for Chrissakes. Dimi!

★

Dimi finds him face down in the ditch outside the saloon. He goes to move him and the drunk pushes with his left arm at the air.

Pop, let's go.

The drunk swats blindly at the air again.

How much money you lose at the backgammon board, heh Pop?

The drunk shakes his head and says: Go on . . .

What'd they take you for in there?

Go on now . . .

He reaches underneath and flips his father. He steadies him on his forearms. And then he hoists the drunk onto his sinewy back amid slurred protests.

Let's go, Pop. You're done.

When he gets to the mayor's house, he puts down the drunk to rest a bit. He wipes his forehead with his arm: Chrissakes . . .

Don't take the Lord's name in vain, slurs his father.

The half-starved young Dimi looks down the muddy road, toward the valley where peasants have gathered hay into rolled stacks and the earth looks pockmarked from overplanting.

It's not easy to live altogether in the spirit while you're not fully grown and lobotomized by the church, Pop.

But the drunk doesn't hear him. He's passed out again and snores with horrendous impunity.

★

From the top of the stairs by the front door she can see him running way out in the distance. He is coming home from the edge of the forest and at first all she can see is his long, dirty blonde hair swinging in the wind, except there is no wind and she thinks Lord he must really be running fast.

Hooligan, she says out loud still standing there squinting and slowly inching up on her toes.

She thinks: He's done something bad for sure. Something really bad if he's running like that and this time I'm not saving him from anything. I just hope he didn't set fire to the forest, is what I hope. That he didn't set no fire to no forest. Ah, he's gonna get a beating when he gets here. A big one, too.

Dimi! What's that you're running from, boy. Heh?

The boy is closer now, still running hard and fast and as she squints harder and takes her hand to the forehead to cut the glare, she sees something big and white running after him. Flying, it's FLYING after him. Now it's running again.

Hey old man, she yells to the backyard. Come here and look at something. I can't see too good.

He doesn't hear her. He's splitting wood with a thick axe and when she yells to him he is coming down hard on a piece. Her words get lost in the sharp *crrrrack*.

Old man, she tries again, come see your son . . . then she cocks her head and squishes her face together to get a better look. The boy is much closer, still running full speed, still chased by a big white, sometimes-flying, sometimes-running, something.

Oh Jesus, she says exploding with laughter and puts her hands on her hips.

Come see your son old man, she yells again. Come see what he's running from you ol' deaf fool you. Put that axe down and come now.

She walks to the gate and looks down the street and here he comes now like a crazy devil, hair still fluttering, mouth wide open, tears running down his dirty cheeks, looking back to see if it's gained any ground, and it has, because it can go airborne and its long neck is bent forward aerodynamically and it's making a hissing sound like a snake and it's almost got him by the pants now, almost, just a little closer and the boy looks back at it again and begins to cry loudly because he knows that anytime now this angry goose is going to catch him and kill him, probably bite him to death.

Maaaaaaa, open the gate, he yells but she barely hears him for her laughter and before he gets to the house he trips on a large rock and tumbles on the hard, gravel road while the goose breaks off the pursuit and settles down, hissing and flapping his wings at the derailed, weeping boy.

★

When she opens her eyes it's a quarter to five. She shifts slowly and props herself up on her good side and looks at the small clock ticking loudly on the nightstand beside her bed. It says five-thirty.

Jeeesus, you were some scoundrel, she says. You and that blasted goose.

What goose, Ma?

She pats down her permed, gray hair.

Mmmyea.

Ma?

Look here. In the back room there's a small suitcase. It's locked.

There's some money in there for you, Dimi.

Ma?

Go ahead. Your father hid it in there for twenty-five years. Half his pension's worth. Put it in there every month, the old fool. Drank the rest. In the back room. Go ahead.

What, Ma?

Take the money. The suitcase. In the back room, Dimi.

Ma, there's no back room.

Eh no back room. Let me at it.

And she swings herself to the side of the bed, her feet reaching for the slippers on the floor. The factory across the river blows its whistle. She says: Third shift's over.

And then: Remember how hard we laughed when we buried your father?

Tea's ready.

What was her name? That woman who always showed up and cried at funerals . . .

Barna.

That's it. Remember? Father Georg dumped vinegar into the wine bottle to teach her a lesson. Eh?

23

She explodes with an asthmatic laugh, which degrades into a bout of coughing.

Jeeesus that was something, she says. To see her face pucker up like that, the mooch . . .

Tea's ready, Ma.

That devil of a woman. She ended up drinking the entire bottle. Out of spite.

And she starts laughing again, patting down her hair.

★

I had a strange dream.

Did you.

Of your father.

Well now.

He was standing on the bank of the Danube and I was on the other side, the water separating us and running hard. He kept smiling and waving for me to come over. He kept saying come on now, just . . . come on, don't be afraid. Come on, sweetheart.

He never called you sweetheart.

Mmmyea. Maybe one time . . .

He didn't.

. . . and I kept saying NO NO NO I don't know how to swim, but he was smiling and waving me over the bloody Danube and I was saying, you old deaf fool, didn't you hear me? I don't know how to swim. Except he wasn't old, he was like I knew him before we were married, and he was just standing there, and then he opened his arms wide and said Look! Look at this! Look at me, Marie! And then I woke up.

The Danube.

Oh for Chrissakes Dimi, when are you going to stop smoking?

★

Your grandson is getting married.

Jeeesus Dimi, why didn't you tell me?

I just did, Ma. He's written you a letter. He says he wishes you had a telephone so he could tell you himself.

Like father like son with the blasted telephone, she smiles and looks at the icon of Jesus imparting mercy with his palms up. When you were a boy you used to ask me how it was that they took a picture of Jesus. You know, way back then when there was were no cameras.

When I was a boy you used to tell me you and Pop hid needles into the mattress so I wouldn't bounce on it.

She laughs.

It worked.

Mmmyea, he mocks her.

She laughs.

You were something, Dimi . . .

Was I now.

She swipes at the air, still laughing: Don't be a scoundrel. Days are getting shorter.

★

When she opens her eyes it's a quarter to five. She shifts slowly and looks at the small clock ticking loudly on the nightstand beside her bed. It says five-thirty. She's always set her clocks forty-five minutes ahead. She lifts up a bit on her left elbow.

What're you doing over there. I can't see you, what're you doing. What is that.

The man in the doorway takes a half step into the cold room.

Oh for Chrissakes, you old fool. What have you got on. What have you got there.

Only the man is not old. He's maybe twenty. And he's wearing an army uniform with epaulets on his shoulders. His hair is slicked back with pomade and his shoes are shiny from having been rubbed and buffed with paraffin.

You old fool, she says and rights herself up onto the side of the bed. She goes fumbling for her glasses on the nightstand and knocks over the small Jesus icon.

What have you gone and done to yourself now . . .

She pats down her hair and blinks the room into focus. For Godsakes man, what're you doing with that get up on. You old crazy fox. Where'd you find that old getup anyway.

The officer steps back into the doorway. And then he steps back farther and turns and goes through the heavy dark curtain of cold into the ante-room.

Wait a minute, for Chrissakes . . . you deaf bull. Did you hear? Wait a minute, I'll go unlock the valise for you. Get your money out of there . . .

She pushes and lifts into her slippers. She shivers in the morning air and goes across, toward the ante-room. When she steps through the French doors, she pauses and reaches around for the tie to the bathrobe that she's left on the bed. She thinks of something for a second, changes her mind, and then crosses into the dark ante-room.

Hold your horses, man. There's the matter of the ration to the village cooperative this month. And then there's feeding the animals . . .

BASIL

I SEE HIM from time to time walking around town.

Do you now.

Yes. With a little leather satchel.

That's him all right.

Funny, he doesn't look like a father. Much less *your* father.

The man with the jet-black hair laughs.

Yea well . . . it's just recessive genes. Nothing I can do.

Do you know what I mean, though?

I do.

He's just this . . . he doesn't look like your father. He doesn't look like any other immigrant pensioner I know.

When's the last time you saw him?

I don't remember the day really. I was having a coffee outside Lido and he rushed by. He had on earbuds but they didn't seem connected to anything. I could see the jack hanging there. He looked very resolute.

The man with the jet-black hair laughs again.

That's him all right.

But, do you know what I mean? He doesn't . . . it's like he's not a father. He's something else. Doesn't belong here. You know?

I do. And it's true.

It's like he's Gandhi or something. Walking on water or hot coals or something. Scarred.

They both laugh.

You know, I got him a Tomish, the man with jet black hair says.

What?

A Tomish meter. A pedometer.

Oh. What'd you say?

A pedometer.

No, what'd you call it the first time?

A Tomish meter. I think it's named for Thomas Jefferson, who invented it.

Gandhi with a pedometer. From America, no less. Via Bulgaria.

Un-connected earbuds . . .

And a leather satchel with God knows what inside.

They both laugh.

I swear to God, there's just . . . something about him. Calming. Soothing. All that walking. It's like he's not your father. Do you know what I mean?

★

Dad? Dad.

The little, brown man doesn't look at him. He has one small earphone with a very long cord attached to the television. The cord traverses a chair, a dining table, and the length of the room before it dead-ends into a hole just below the screen. The wire is taut and it's pulling the earphone out, slightly.

Dimi?

No. Dad, it's me.

Dimi?

No Dad. It's me.

The man rubs on his knuckle.

Did you write to Nadia? he says.

Yes. Dad?

Tell Mikki he needs to call the World Bank.

All right. Dad, do you know who I am?

The man pushes hard on the earphone, adjusts it back into the canal, and then clears his throat.

Dimi, we have to get your mother to start exercising, he says. She's type 2. You know that. We have to get her moving. Her heart.

It's me, Dad. Your son.

How did you get here? The car?

No.

Who has the car?

Bloody everyone, that's who. Everyone in the goddamn city has it.

Aha.

Did that come out loud? It doesn't seem to matter. It doesn't look like his father heard any of it.

Four miles a day Dimi, the man says. At least four. At least. Ten thousand steps. Eight kilometers. What's that . . . that's what? In miles . . . He reaches for his pedometer on the couch pillow next to him and clicks the reset button.

Five.

Five, the man says. It takes discipline, Dimi.

I'm not Dimi.

No. Dimi's dead.

That's right, Dad. Dimi's dead.

Aha.

He doesn't want to be here. He doesn't want to see his father this way. The old man keeps rubbing at his knuckle. Looks toward the balcony. Then back to the screen. Two monkeys are copulating. It's a nature show of some sort. The male is very fast. Extremely fast.

They throw cow parts in the rubbish, the old man says. Before eight at night.

What?

Cow parts. The ones they don't eat. The scraps.

Who? Who throws them?

The gypsies. They poison them. Dip them in Borax.

He won't fight him on this. Not now. He'll let the gypsies take one for the team. This day only. It takes the flak off of him.

We're the ones to blame, the old man says.

That's right, Dad.

Bullshit. Don't talk to me this way.

All right. Should I put on some tea?

No. It will just make me go to the washroom.

All right.

All right.

Do you want to try to walk outside for a bit? Before it gets dark.

Not today, the man says and re-adjusts his earphone. Sometimes there's garlic smells coming through the vents. From other units. And I think they're listening to me. Like back home.

I'll talk to them about it.

Will you?

Before I leave. Maybe they need to change the filters.

The man pushes buttons on his pedometer. Looks toward the balcony. He says: Never let them open you up like they did your mother, on that table.

I know, Dad.

Once they open you up, nothing but bad things happen.

I know.

They sit in silence for a while. Both far away.

Rommie said he saw you walk by Lido's, Dad.

When?

I don't know. Recently. He doesn't know for sure.

Aha.

The man fusses with his pedometer.

Dad, are you using crossings. And waiting at red lights?

He doesn't want to be here.

Are you? Dad.

Yes, I'm waiting.

Are you?

Yes, yes.

Because you have those earbuds jammed into your ears, is all. And you sometimes don't pay attention …

I know. Don't worry. I'm waiting at lights before I cross. Don't worry.

The old man jams his earphone deeper into the canal. He scratches at the other lobe.

Dad, what were you doing all the way by Lido's?

When?

When Rommie saw you.

When was that?

I don't know. Last week maybe.

I don't know. What was I doing?

Walking. That's what he says.

That's what I was doing?

Yes.

Well, then that's what I was doing.

Yes, but why? What's there for you to do so far from here? The old man hits the remote. A confrontation on a reality show. Hits it again. An infomercial for some facial cream. Again. Back to the confrontation.

Dad?

There's not enough pickling in the cabbage leaves at Razva's.

What?

Ninety-nine per cent of restaurants don't pickle their cabbage long enough. Did you know that?

Dad?

I would love some stuffed cabbage. Can you run out and get some? Son. Take my pedometer. It'll show you how long you've walked.

★

The way I get in is, I jump the fence out back. The chain-link. Out back by the stinking garbage and dumpsters. It's tall, 15 feet, but I climb it anyway. They keep the back door to the place open, so if you can scale the fence, then you can come in. That's how I get into the bar. I don't have identification. Well,

I do, but I'm not of age yet. Tavi doesn't care. He owns the place, could get in trouble, but he doesn't care. He doesn't want to know how I get in, just as long as I don't go in through the front door. My money's as good as any other ordinary drunk's. It's how I get in. Scale the chain-link fence out back. And in any case, they're all students from the polytechnic. The people who drink here. They're all students anyway. They have fake identification. The ones who're underage. Tomorrow I have to go visit my father. Check up on him. Rommie said he saw him around here sometime last week, walking. He had on earphones but they weren't plugged into anything. Crossed the street up and back and up and back.

For twenty minutes.

For twenty minutes.

Straight.

This place is a half hour by trolley from his unit. I got to go and see if he's all right. He shouldn't get on the trolley. He shouldn't get on anything. Once, he was locked inside a metro train car overnight, in the rail yard. He fell asleep in the cubby out back, by where they steer the thing, and the mechanic didn't see him—he was behind a blacked-out Plexiglas window—so the engineers backed up the train into the yard and locked him in for the night.

You'll never guess who I saw on the Red Line today. Go ahead. You'll never guess. Go ahead.

I don't know, Dad.

Brezhnev. Eh? Eh? Brezhnev!

Once, he followed who he thought was Pablo Neruda from Unity Plaza all the way down to the old Central Committee complex.

He stomped over my foot, that lousy Chilean.

What?

With his wingtips. With his fancy Italian wingtips. That's not even his real name, Neruda. Did you know that, Dimi?

Dad.

Fancy wingtips, that louse. He drives a Ferrari, you know. Some communist.

★

You have to go see him.

I know.

I don't know what he was doing walking all the way down here; he shouldn't be wandering away from the apartment.

I know, I know.

Will you find out?

He won't tell me.

Why?

He won't remember.

★

I walk. I walk everywhere. I walk toward it. Most people walk away from it. Run, even. I don't mind. I walk toward it. I hope to meet it halfway. Remove the surprise. It. It could be anything or anyone. It could be the milkman, although there are no more milkmen. I had a picture from Life magazine once, of a milkman delivering his bottles among the ruins of London, during the war. He had slicked back hair and it was parted. The picture was alive. He had a look of concentration on his face, as he stepped around piles of rocks and rubble. To deliver the daily milk. To whomever was still living among the ruins. In London. Nineteen forty-something.

It.

It could be the little girl with the red balloon. For Hemingway it was that Englishman, Compton, in a tweed jacket, piloting that little plane above the Kilimanjaro. For Kolatkar it was Jejuri. I don't mind. I walk. Not because of the doctor. I don't care too much for what the doctor says. I don't pay much attention to my statistics. Heart rate. Cholesterol levels, good and bad. Blood pressure. Blood sugar. My wife was alive before the doctor, and after she was dead. So I don't place too much in what he says. He opened her up on the table for a quadruple bypass. And that was her end.

I walk. My son bought me a pedometer. It records paces. Steps. It records them by detecting the motion of the hips. I walk. Sometimes I get on the Metro, so I can then walk. It seems strange, taking public transportation so you can walk. Sometimes I go to his town to make sure he's all right. He lives a 30-minute trolley ride away. I walk the streets around his apartment. I don't know why. It makes me feel good. Like I am his caretaker. I can protect him. I can still protect him. I have a Walkman. I love Vangelis.

Vangelis and Jon Anderson. I love Giorgio Moroder as well. I have to tell you. Walking toward death is liberating. I cannot tell you. But I have to tell you. Walking toward death is liberating.

Here comes my son now.

Dad? Dad? Dad. It's me.

I hear him but I don't hear him. I cannot explain. In my head I'm talking to him. But I know I'm not. Really. I can see it on his face. I'm just his poor father. I'm just looking at him confused. But I'm not. I cannot explain. I wish I could take away his hurt. His pain. Guilt, probably. He's just a boy. Only a boy, really. He's nineteen years of age. Motherless. Fatherless.

★

There are black and white photographs in a shoebox I keep under the bed. When I remember, I take them out. Here's your mother and I in 1962. Before Nadia came around. We are at a party. We are both smoking. I am wearing a suit. She is still overweight. Always has been. This is when we used to travel. When she could, easily. We stayed in an apartment on the coast of the Black Sea. This photo was taken at a party in Sofia. Your mother had Prussian blood. And Lebanese. You and your sister were born in the country. She went to Moscow. You wanted to study there also, but by then we had moved and needed money. You wanted to go. But by then we had gone to that village where the gypsies put you upside down into a rubbish pile. I have always felt remorse for bringing you to that village.

Dad. Let's get you up.

I started walking after Nadia left to chase that man from Libya. And after they moved to South Africa and he had an illegitimate child with that African woman, your mother decided she could not travel anymore. You were always put ahead of everything. You were a boy, and boys are always put ahead of everything. It is why your sister ran away to the bottom of the world. In our household she did not matter as much as you. Your mother knew that's why Nadia left. So did I. It was our culture. I have many regrets. It is what happens to a man who lives too long. He looks back and sees the many regrets. Are you listening? How can you? I am not saying anything to you. I know I'm not. I can see it on your face. I wish I could take away your pain. There are many things I now wish. One of them is to leave here.

Dad?
Don't hold up supper for me.

★

I say this and I turn on my side, facing the wall.

PATROL
(Published in The Adroit Journal, 2015)

THAT'S NOT WAR out there come to the barracks, though clearly it's the sound of ferum screaming through the atmosphere. That's iron to you and me. Atomic number 26. Whistling Dixie as it scratches out a parabolic sound curve through the air. That's 78.09% nitrogen, 20.95% oxygen, 0.93% argon, and throw in a smidgen of carbon dioxide, mm-hmm. Metal bed guts shaking it is, then. It's settled. That's the noise bleeding through the dreamworld. Sounds like the bowels of an inside-rusted saltimbanque are rebelling from too much spoiled waste flowing through, making its way downward. (Man first rots from the organs out to the skin, then to society.)

In focus, it's . . . S-Slothie leaning in, severely altering Lt. (O-2) Bradshaw's depth of field. Slothie: Private, first class . . . lowercase f lowercase c. Leather face, gaunt, pomade heavy in hair (Murray's, $2.89 per 3 oz., circa 1926) a la Burt Lancaster in that seminal war movie with Ol' Blue Eyes as Maggio. The metal springs of his own bed moaning at the insisting pressure of the Pfc. merrily jolt O-2 Bradshaw into this reality. The Now. Christ, the Lt. says, just in time, Slothie. Patrol sir, the first class (lowercase f lowercase c) pomade pushes out, breath heavy with smoke and faux cheese. How in hell did he have time to grab breakfast? And a cigarette. Patrol ASAP, he says again, now a whiff of green onion and radishes sneaking out of his nostrils. Christ, what they're passing off for chow nowadays. Why so alarmed, Slothie, Bradshaw rubbing crust from his eyes and dried spittle from the sides of his lips. It must've been a raucous night for the sinuses. Imagine the moaning. Imagine the morning. He runs his tongue over his teeth. Over nasty film. (Film at seven/eleven.) Plaque's got your tongue? Jesus Slothie, why so ambitious. It's barely morning. Isn't it. Pomade Slothie as Mother Superior. Pomade as worrier. Pomade as warrior. You'll never guess ol' Slothie what kind of dream you've pulled me from. Go ahead, I'll give you two shots then you're out. But Mother Superior pushes on with this patrol routine, pulling at the O-2's clavicle and delivering all the news that's fit to (s)print.

Bradshaw sucks his teeth, large-ish morsels of last night's mess hall slop drawn in from between the crevices and down the pipe tumbling into an abyss of gastric acid. That's a composition of hydrochloric acid, potassium chloride, and sodium chloride to you and me, chum. Any chance at a new toothbrush from the supply room, Slothie? Need those stiff bristles for *this* job. The entire squad now warming up like lizards from the un-nerving night lets out a big, cohesive laugh followed by savage morning noises coming from awakening orifices, organs, machinery. There's that metal screech again, though now Bradshaw has established that they all need new beds. Or a good lube from a tub of WD-40. Amigos, nobody get up suddenly or the Komandant'll think the spooks are lobbing mortars onto the barracks.

Who the hell's in charge here anyway.

Ain't it you.

There's paperwork to go with this. Always paperwork, says Bradshaw climbing into his Army Combat Uniform (ACU). Flak jacket: check. Name tapes: check. Rank insignia: check. IR IFF squares sewn to shoulders to help identify friendlies when night vision devices are used: check. Wait just a cotton-pickin' minute, this is a day patrol innit?

Slothie, remind me to tell you the alternate reality from which you woke me. Something to do with a crucifixion, making a French delicacy with twenty-five layers of pig intestines, and a suicide bomber whose detonation device triggers a spewing out of confetti instead. Helluva dream or parallel universe if you ask me. Only the P to f to the c is gone. Probably slipping into his own A to the C to the U: OGIO flak jacket, 1950CU . . . good ol' Rocinante, standard U.S. Army issue. You can ride *that* to Parnassus, mm-hmm.

★

Outside the Green Zone everything is brown. Will you look at that, Cim Boldo now, staff sergeant, peeking out the hole of the HMMWV. ("Mobility Solutions for Cost-Effective Client Needs") Don't listen to him. Keep your eyes on the . . . what is this anyway, says Bradshaw to the driver. It's an RHD, sir. Right-Hand-Drive Humvee. Jesus Age Christ, what are we patrolling here Sutton-in-Ashfield? Who the hell ordered this vehicle backwards like this? Cim Boldo the Historian inserts a wad of dip into his lower gum and laughs: maybe the *Eye*-talians. Ya know driving on the left side o' the road comes from ze Romans, dontcha. They found that tracks pon the left-hand side leading into towns wuz deeper than them there coming out o' them, pon ze right. Meaning? Meaning: shit was being carried in. Heavier loads in the carts. All them keeping to the left. Carts coming out of towns were empty. Shallower tracks. All them keeping to the right, suh. And then, changing vibes, Cim Boldo cogitates: Everything is solid brown dontcha know. Shit brown. But shittier. Like war shittier. Brown like the corduroys your mama stuffed you in back in Missoula in

'76. Brown like Buster Brown shoes. 'Member those? Got 'em out of the Sears catalogue every September. Don't listen to him. Keep your eyes on the road, says Bradshaw to the melancholic driver who's homesick for the yearly mailer Richard Sears first used to advert watches and jewelry in that 1888 Book o' Bargains. A Money Saver for Everyone. Keep your eyes on the road, private.

Is that what this is. A road.

Organization of the patrol: two fire teams of four soldiers each; the squad leader is typically a sergeant or corporal, only Bradshaw rides with them this time so he gives out the orders instead. Locotenente is how Cim Boldo spins it, *tenente* for short. (Boldo must have a thing for the *Eye*-talians.) That suits Bradshaw just fine. As long as everyone's got their minds on the IEDs and the IEDs on their minds. So merrily they go along, hop-skipping through the Helmand province north toward Lashkar Gah.

At Bost Airport *ze panzer* stops on the service road to jettison three saps with bursting bladders. Relief comes to each in the form of a green, rolling meadow—a suspect oasis in the middle of a brown lunarscape, a steppe peppered by trapezoidal fields of dead locoweed and land mines. *Aaah . . .* (Flushing Meadows, ahahaha . . .)

What kind of name is Slothie? Dimitri (from Paris) playing cultural anthropologist with his pimmel in his hand. Short for Slothberg. From the mother country. You mean you ain't slow like that . . . monkey creature, Cannonball Adderall, the other Pfc. taking care to piss with the wind. For that comment, he extracts a backhand cross the shoulder blades. Jewish then, Dimitri playing the *ignorant* cultural anthropologist. From Paree.

Slothie to Cannonball: Mind your stream, amigo. To Dimitri: No, German.

Jesus Age, Bradshaw bellowing through the porthole of the panzer. He sticks out a hair-singed forearm and points at a wristwatch. The pissing squad pushes to finish out the job, knowing full well they're out in the open like quacking ducks. But there is always that little bit left in the bladder. That little bit that haunts a man's psyche an hour down the road. That's what the squad is dribbling out now in various stages of success. Under duress. A mess.

So it's out once again, faces morose with boredom and the realization that walking in Alexander the Great's footsteps ain't all it's cracked up to be, no matter what the CO said at that meeting back in the Land of the Free, the Home of the Brave.

Bradshaw looks 'round at the faces of his patrol squad, heads bobbing in comical unison: yessuh yessuh. What? Yessuh yessuh. A bigger band of discontent half- and adopted brothers he hasn't seen. They could all be double-agents. *At least* double-agents. Yees, you're down here now, down here with us. Get your sniffles and your shame out now. Get them out the way, young fellas. Because we don't make a practice of indulging *that* for too long. Cannonball Adderall would like the all-you-can-eat extravaganza at the Red Lobster in Grand Island. Is that over by the Platte River in that Nebraska, Slothie hears Bradshaw pinging 'round the neurons on the inside, only the *tenente* doesn't actually move his mouth. What the hell now, they can all communicate extrasensory like? Rily? No, really. Dimitri (from Paris) is melancholic for the days he sang in a barbershop quartet in Skokie, Illinois. A capella. *Eye*-talian for in chapel style. Oh what I'd give to sing again in costume. Cim Boldo scoffs, you ain't got no skills for the second harmonic, never mind heterodyning, kiddo. And holy shit, thinks Cannonball Adderall who's just heard the back and fro between the staff sarge and the Pfc., they really can all communicate extrasensory like. E to the S to the P.

★

It's a sack of shit, is what it is, says the driver pulling up to the burlap irregular mass left in the middle of a nowhere road. Maybe it's potatoes, Slothie feeling a bit Pavlovian. A bit Watsonian. Feeling a bit tingly in the taste buds. Back home in Crappalachia, Uncle Cliffie'd slice them tubers all up with his hunting knife and dump 'em into an iron pan crackling with oil, mmm. But Watson's experiments back then in the Jazz Age with that lil' Albert cherub who wasn't afraid of no ghost, no rats either, yielded something else: classical conditioning as the impetus for phobias. Elementary, my dear Pavlov. So now Slothie is afraid. Paranoia sneaks up the femurs and into the hips. From there she's off for the spaces and the tangents and the hidden crevices.

The war boys get out. Our usual suspects: S-Slothie, Lt. Bradshaw, Cim Boldo, and Cannonball Adderall. Hold on to your scrotums, fellas. This might be a booby-trap job.

High angle, establishing shot, omniscient point of view: brown, camo-ed Humvee in the middle of [motherfucking] nowhere Helmand province purring next to four saps PokingProbing, poking, probing the sinister contents of a brown sack left on a road half a click southwest of Gereshk. We're ready for a close-up, Mr. DeMille. And so down we crane for a better look. And a better hear.

The hell.

It's soft-lookin'. Squishy-like maybe.

Watch for clear fishing gut.

Jesus Age, this ain't the movies.

Slothie's fantasy of potatoes *au gratin* squashed now by an intolerable cruelty of the present. The bitter, dry end of his psychic reflex. End of the road for Pavlov. Cim Boldo draws a mental short straw, steps up and opens the fetid pouch. Clearly he's repulsed. Surely, Shirley.

The fuck, O-2 Bradshaw peering inside at the mess. Jesus Age. And head retracts all turtle-like.

Hell is it.

The hell is it is a person is what it is. Broken down in segments of scantily covered bare bone. Crushed, mutated-like. It's a woman. Was, more like it. There's the hair. There's a leg. Hey Henry here's a wing.

Bloody shit, Cim Boldo now. Lookin' like someone took a sledgehammer to her. Slothie steps in and clarifies: it's a stoning. They stoned her. Dead. Dead-dead-good, all right. The savages.

And then it comes: *Bijjjjou*. It's small and quick and hits dead on, lickety-split. They all see it but the first second after it happens, the image doesn't make it 'cross all the axons to register true meaning. To the boys it looks like a rock. Someone from inside *ze panzer* musta thrown a rock at S-Slothie's helmet and hit 'im square on. *Hey man, nice shot*. Helmet spasms and dents and Slothie feels like God's giant index finger done just poked him in the back of the noggin. Zip, zip, zip, the electrical impulses now making quick sense of the sniper bullet that just said Hello Boyz Howya Doin Michael Corleone Says Hello.

High angle, omniscient point of view: four ants scrambling back to an iron box on inflatable rubber wheels, spewing gliding metal, cupronickel, copper alloys, and steel whistling through the air. Jacketed lead. That's bullets intended for higher-velocity applications to you and me, chum.

Jesus Age, *tenente* Bradshaw inside the HMMWV. ("Mobility Solutions for Cost-Effective Client Needs") Lucky as shit they're using low-caliber pebbles. Prolly a 6.5 Grendel. Or a 6.8 SPC . . .

Funny. P to the f to the c Hans S-Slothberg doesn't *feel* lucky as shit. But maybe that's just Pavlovian paranoid pessimism.

Dissolve to, high angle: ze panzer disintegrating into the brown lunarscape as the fellas inside sing.

Way-ell it's a darned good life and it's kinda funny
How the Lord made the bee and the bee made the honey
An' the honeybee lookin' for a home
An' they called it Honeycomb
Got a hank o' hair and a piece o' bone
Way-ell honeycomb won't ya be mah baby
Way-ell honeycomb won't ya be mah own

Fade to black.

THE DECADENCE OF WESTERN CULTURE: BEVERLY HILLS, CALIFORNIA OR DOWN-N-OUT IN VALHALLA

THE FOLLOWING ACCOUNT was received from our friend inside the Writers Guild of America (West) after attending an industry "wrap" party concluding the debut season of a drama titled "NYPD Blue."

He sang this a bit sharp:

If you're really feeling low
and you've got no one you know . . .
Sad, sad storay.
Then the world begins to shine
like you had-a-too much wine . . .
that's amore.

But seriously, (he snapped his head toward the pool) you gotta go see him. He'll set you straight no matter what. He's a fuckin' genius like that. Genius. I mean it, like. Like Eisenstein or some shit.

Einstein, I said. Eisenstein was a different guy.

Just . . . fuckin' do me a favor and go talk to him.

Him was a long-haired, long-bearded yogi in a Speedo swimsuit and nothing else. This was Beverly Hills. I had arrived here by mistake. A mis-delivered invite. Wrong door. Wrong life. Right time.

In February, I broke down in El Segundo and left the car on the 405 for the rats to lift it to a chop shop and make a profit on whatever parts there was a profit to be made. I walked through abandoned oil fields and vacant lots and hooked up with two heroin addicts and a teenage male prostitute in North Hollywood. We ended up sharing a broken-down tenement unit off Irvine and Vanowen.

I worked as a short order cook at Bennigan's and picked up freelance videography gigs from old, retired film executives rotting away from dementia in Laguna Beach. *I was AP on Sunset Boulevard. Goddamit all to hell, I was.* They always started a conversation the same way: *Back in those days . . .*

Eight bucks an hour from these rich geriatric fucks. In Los Angeles, in the early 90s you couldn't buy a pack of toilet paper with the weekly I pulled in. Never mind now.

You gotta gat? Own one like is what I mean? Legal or illegal although illegal would be best. Untraceable and all that. A forty-four maybe. Forty-four Magnum. You know what a forty-four Magnum can do to a man's balls? You should see that. That you should see. You should see what a forty-four Magnum can do to a man's balls. Although nobody carries a forty-four anymore. Goddamn only Harry Callahan yea? Well fuck Harry Callahan if you ask me. Fuck him. Yea. How's that Harry. I just made your day. All the kids pack nine millimeters now. Still. Forty-four man. Old days. Old times. Pull that out and the rats scurry. Guaranteed. Haha. Gay-rohn-teed. You know how that cat says it on the TV. You know?

The yogi. He talked like a Tommy gun. And in perfect American English. Wicked are the men who dispense enlightenment from the side of the pool, clad only in aquamarine skivvies.

No. I don't have a TV.

Jesus. Really.

Yea.

You gotta have a gat at least though. Gotta. It's life in the big city baby. You ain't shit without a gat. Correction. You can't *do* shit without a gat. Seriously. I'm serious.

I'm from DC. I didn't need a gun there, I said.

DC. Ha. East Coast. Politicians. Ha. Pansies. What you need a gat for there anyway. Won't do you no good. Them DC fuckers kill you with bills.

He re-lit his joint. The ash fell on his bare belly.

I don't know. There's some tough motherfuckers on the East Coast.

He thought about it.

Who's the president now? Hoover?

To be decided.

Yea, right. And then you woke up. What do you drive like anyway?

What?

Wheels. What kind of car do you drive?

I don't have one.

Ha. Kid. This is Los Angeles. Kid. You ain't shit without a car in Los Angeles. A car and a gat. And a fuckin' TV. Will you? Will you get yourself a fuckin' TV for Chrissakes.

He took a long drag. Then offered it to me. I burned it down to my fingertips. I gave it back.

Where you from originally? You talk funny.

I told him.

He waited and dragged down on the roach until his fingers turned black.

Fantastic then. I'll set you up with a balalaika. Make you feel at home. Can you use one?

What?

A balalaika. Can you use a balalaika?

What, you mean like play?

Play, use. Yea.

I don't know . . . I can't play . . .

Fantastic. You call me, I'll set you up with one.

I don't have a phone.

Call from a payphone. Get my number from Uncle Milti. Go ahead man.

Who's Uncle Milti?

The yogi laughed. Two girls were leaving. He moved his foot into their path and looked them down and smiled at them.

The guy who put on the party. You don't know Uncle Milti? Everybody knows Uncle Milti. Go ahead now.

Yea.

Call me okay? I'll set you up with a balalaika. Don't forget.

All right.

He didn't move. I took it that he was done with me. I turned to leave.

Get yourself a gat, East Coast. You need one. I don't care where you're from. I don't care where you lived. AC, DC . . . Seriously. Man, seriously. You taking me serious? Heh?

Yea.

You gonna do it. Right? Tell me you gonna do it. Go ahead. Tell me. Right?

All right.

My boy. That's my *boy* right there. Welcome to Hollywood baby. You gonna be a big star.

A PURSUIT RACE
(Published in The Stockholm Review of Literature, 2015)

THE CURIOSITY ON THE semi-circular horizon vacillated between the shape of a small, vertical line and a semicolon. It must surely be an optical illusion of a simple rock formation or the parasitic cone of the volcano itself, Paasili thought and then he screamed. Nothing up here echoed. Nothing ever replied to his periodic howling requests. It had become a farce, the calling out, but he kept it up almost by habit. It was hope of sorts. The heat rolled in regiments made from broiling iron that advanced into the body like the horns of a feral, saddled bull. The waves of murderous heat formed a weird, giant lens through which everything danced and undulated. Paasili fixed on the shape again. Now it was split into three very short segments and had changed to a horizontal position like an unstable ellipsis shaking with either fear or rage. The curiosity seemed to be moving clockwise toward him rapidly.

It's impossible to be even afraid, Paasili thought. Nothing lives up here. Nothing has ever lived up here. The black earth that soiled his shoes was sometimes muddy and thick like a hot paste and other times dry and powdery, depending on which side of the circumferential crater he found himself. He checked the shape again. It was most definitely in motion, coming around like an opponent in a cycling pursuit race.

A shiv would be helpful to have now, Paasili thought and touched all around his waist feeling even inside at the gusset to confirm he wasn't carrying anything that could be fashioned into a weapon to defend himself. In the worst case, he thought, I'll feign nervousness and push him into the throat of the fiery mountain. But why did he think the curiosity was a man? It could be a dog or a parched hyena or a forgotten sister hurrying to bring cheese and water. It could be anything—from nothing could be created everything—a semicolon, an ellipsis. God created everything from nothing.

Even a semicolon! Paasili shouted but did not await an echo. He walked faster, away from the pursuing entity but losing ground. How helpful a shiv could have been, still.

For as long as he could remember, Paasili had lived on the crater of the volcano. He had no memory of a childhood. For as long as he was aware, he walked the rim of the fiery mountain. Continuously. Perpetually. Years ago, he would pinch various parts of his underarm throughout the day or cut into his thigh with cooled but sharp volcanic rocks in order to violently awaken himself from what he thought was a Sisyphean dream. But all that rendered was a series of wounds and scratches that would take an unusually long time to heal. Because of the heat, blood couldn't coagulate and form a proper crust. That's what he conjured as an explanation.

He had no idea when he was born or by whom. In the time spent on the volcano, which now seemed neither long nor short, Paasili formed certain inflexible thoughts about his own character: he fancied himself a chivalrous romantic and a lover of all animals. He was sure were he ever to meet either a woman or, say, a defenseless hare in search of fresh clover on the unfortunate scorched earth of the crater, he would offer everything that a chivalrous, romantic man—a lover of all animals—would be expected to provide. Though he didn't truly know what that would be. Nor was he sure if he would be able to recognize a hare.

Another look askance at the pursuing curiosity filled Paasili with a strange melancholy for not ever having had anything against which to measure his chivalry, courage, or kindness. He was an untried, incomplete man. He wasn't sure he would ever die, and that made him well up with further anger at the futility of his condition and situation. He decided he would use the curiosity, soon, to catch up to his hurried pace, as a scapegoat for his discontent and failures. Yes, he would feign innocence and nervousness when confronted, and simply shove it down the main vent into the magma chamber, no matter what it was or what it wanted.

From the cloud of toxic steam into which Paasili was about to enter (hoping to hide from the ever-closing curiosity in order that he may ambush it and crush its head with a rock), a long, sinewy shape dislodged and halted to ascertain the situation before him. Paasili had never encountered a living being on the rim of the crater before, and upon seeing this emaciated lad he urinated a little stream down the leg of his pants, but from the happiness of curiosity and expected interaction, not fear. Fear was expelled the moment Paasili decided to murder whatever it was that was coming for him. The man was a stretched shadow with peculiar, nonlinear burns on his face, especially below the jaw and down his neck. The burns had healed as best the flesh could offer, but the disfigurement provided the man with a menacing look even when not engaged in conflict and, in fact, at ease or relaxing as he seemed to be now.

What is the weather like up ahead, the man asked Paasili. What do you mean weather, Paasili answered. No one has ever asked such a question. No one has ever lived up here, in fact; who are you? The man, despite his contorted face, smiled and excused himself for forgetting his manners. His scarred physiognomy contorted grotesquely from the laborious smile (the cheek grossly invaded the space usually occupied by his left eye and covered it) yet Paasili felt at ease. The man introduced himself as a scout of Prussian descent. A scout for what, Paasili asked. For the fleeing party of refugees coming soon behind me, said the man. I don't understand, Paasili said. No one has ever lived here. No one has ever existed. We are war refugees, the scout said. And historical precedence is none of my concern. I cannot do anything about that. But please excuse my direct manner, the scout said. I don't have very much time and I'm under pressure to lead and report details of the environment to the war refugees' commanding unit. What war, Paasili asked. The war that first started as a game being played with markers and mathematical calculations on an innocent board but then slowly dispersed onto the continents, the scout said. Preposterous, that could be any war, Paasili said.

The scout agreed and laughed; when he shook from chuckling he steadied himself on Paasili's shoulder. Paasili noticed that the man's hands were soft and quite smooth—the opposite of his face—and they smelled like black tobacco and gunpowder. The scout said that Prussians made the most efficient soldiers in the war but also the most perspicacious scouts, and that the history books and the world may have been quite aware of the former but had absolutely no idea of the latter. That is why he was suited to conduct the exploration ahead of the convoy of refugees. Are the scars on your face from battle, Paasili asked. The scout said no. I was born with them just as anyone is born with two arms or two ears. The scout said it didn't bother him that Paasili studied his burns like a map. You may have very well made a competent general, the man said and saluted. Paasili raised his arm and tried to mimic the gesture but could not. He stood with a fist in the air and felt self-conscious and then he also felt like he was being mocked.

What about the weather up ahead, said the scout. It is clear but noxious, Paasili answered. But I suppose you would be used to that by now. Yes, everything is clear but noxious, the scout laughed again but this time did not need the shoulder to steady himself. He was perfectly stable. If you think that, he said and looked at Paasili with one grey eye, wait until you enter the cloud of toxic steam you're headed for. It will make the inside of your throat close in agony. No one can get used to that. Not even some of us who've been gassed. Paasili stood there with his arm raised awkwardly, still not understanding why he couldn't return the scout's salute. His brain wasn't sending the signal. He wasn't worried about the fumes. He had gone through them several hundred times before. They were banded together like quilts and hung everywhere. Are you a Prussian, the scout said. I don't know, Paasili answered. Then more than likely you are. What does that mean, thought Paasili. That doesn't make any sense. This burned lad was certainly the strangest fellow with the most peculiar mannerisms. Now mind your way, as very soon you'll be encountering the convoy, said the scout. Even though it's quite a large party, don't let that intimidate you. Mind your way and let them pass. They will be rushing through with great impunity.

Sidetracked by the details of the abnormal event that had just transpired and the conversation, Paasili forgot about the curiosity in pursuit and as the scout took leave and tended to his duties, Paasili neglected to inform him or warn about the inevitable encounter he was about to have with a semicolon or ellipsis that was following. In addition, he thought about the very certainty of encountering this same scout and the party of refugees on the move at one point again in the future, since the crater, as any crater, was circumferential. Again and again and again and again they would meet. Paasili became amused at the possibility of re-living the same conversation with the scarred man in perpetuity. It could be comical if the same line of discussion would be repeated word for word. The feeling of giddiness that overcame Paasili as he thought of all the available permutations for his future encounters with the man erased his plans of violence perpetrated upon the approaching creature. He was in an incomparably better mood than before. And how long had it been since he'd checked on that strange curiosity? He looked but did not step into the cloud of steam, expecting the convoy of war refugees to emerge at any point now.

They came with the roar of a long night train hauling coal and sand and wounded prisoners. It was a formidable apparition, first emerging from the toxic fog like a victorious but bleeding snake. The line of sleighs pulled by odd, almost miniature horses slid easily on cutter runners that slashed the volcanic soil as if it were freshly fallen, powdery snow. Piled stories high upon the vehicles were objects that seemed burned or irradiated by modern weapons. An entire village was being transported on these odd sleds. Homes and animal coups and barns and outdoor kitchens were balanced expertly, secured with ropes that passed in loops several times from the tops of the structures to the bottoms of the toboggans. Streets and pebbled alleyways had been nestled into the narrow spaces and fissures created by the gargantuan puzzle of material being transported. They stuck out like lances left behind by fallen knights.

Rectangular fields of wheat and corn were geometrically arranged to minimize drag on the vehicles, while the drivers whistled, spat, and swung the whips upon the horses' wet backs, pushing them into a froth-induced haze.

Despite the haste of the convoy, Paasili spotted the charred bodies of those who had fallen as collateral in whatever war they were escaping. There were naked peasants with burned, flappy skin or missing limbs wedged into every available space at the bottom of each passing sleigh. Everything had been taken, it seemed. No spoils were left for the victors. There were women and infants charred beyond recognition, their faces shrunken and reduced to contorted figs. Some had been scalped.

Paasili tried to imagine what was left in place where the village had been: scarred earth, infertile, a massive hole filled with boiling mud and ash, hills like white elephants with gaping, tuskless mouths where defensive positions for machine guns had been dug and abandoned. The victors would come upon nothing that could sustain life. What had they gained after all? What type of territory?

Suddenly from the back of the last sleigh, several objects tumbled out toward Paasili. They looked like big wooden pieces of a brown and red puzzle and as the convoy sped away, Paasili walked toward the strewn material soiled by the viscous mush on the crater.

They were icons—religious scenes painted by hand directly onto thick planks of timber and encased in plywood frames held together at the corners by minuscule nails, buttressed on the inside with rolled-up pages of newspaper. There were painted images of saints with what Paasili identified as some type of golden coronas encircling their heads in a rudimentary, two-dimensional style reminiscent of children's drawings. Paasili laughed at the badly executed gold circles, which were probably meant to be crowns or halos floating above the heads. Each saint was depicted with his hands clasped together in a solemn, trance-like state of repose. In one such representation, Jesus himself was being christened with water by John the Baptist. The scene was comical. John the Baptist's hand, presumably making a gesture of blessing, seemed to be shading Christ from the glare of an unseen sun, providing an amusing visor made of flesh, while with the other he was pouring water from a jug with a long neck like a swan's.

Ridiculous symbols, but something must be done with them, Paasili thought. Some type of respectful entombment must be allowed them. There were no materials to construct a mausoleum or a sepulcher for the icons, so Paasili took to digging with his hands a shallow hole into the sticky, hot mud in order that he could bury the painted wood. But as quickly as he would excavate the material, just as expeditiously the hole would fill itself back up from the bottom. Paasili found this odd, this strange regeneration of the earth, this adamant refusal to receive the icons in a proper way. He worked twice as hard and fast now, digging with both hands joined at the fingers like a dipper shovel on an excavating machine. The work was futile. It yielded nothing but burned flesh and dirty fingernails.

Paasili stood and looked behind at the approaching entity. It was neither a punctuation mark now nor an organism filled with life. The wooden religious objects strewn about angered him. They derailed him. He spat into the steaming soil and picked up the material with disgust. And then, with one swift, violent motion, he heaved the pile of painted wood down the throat of the volcano, into the magma chamber.

And then he turned and faced the approaching entity, now showing its intent clearly. Paasili suddenly became filled with lucidity and purpose. He pointed to the earth all about him.

What kind of place is this, he yelled at the oncoming force. What kind of fucking place is this that you can't even bury the dead.

THE GOOD SENTINEL
(Published in the Rappahannock Review, 2015)

> *The State is the coldest of all cold monsters . . .*
> *And this lie creeps from its mouth:*
> *"I, the state, am the people."*
> *- Nietzsche*

MANY YEARS LATER, as he stepped up to the gallows before a gathered few official spectators in the drafty subterranean parking garage of the Intercontinental Hotel, Damian Meier would feel nostalgic for the days before the revolution. In addition, he would feel remorse for all the things that he had committed to accomplish in his life but had yet remained to be discharged. And myopically, he would feel contrite for the several appointments that were to be abandoned in light of his sudden fate, one of which was a meeting with an attractive woman in the office of a purged Central Committee member to discuss the installation of a wall dividing the grounds of the Athenaeum Opera House from the street. But he would not feel like a worthless animal waiting for his neck to be broken in order that its fur be used for a winter hat. No. That was the kind of thinking for a romantic or a poet. Damian Meier, in the moments he had before he was to be hanged, would simply feel unresolved.

The truth is Damian Meier did not have clear memories of his childhood. He remembered his father and his mother, and sometimes he remembered thunderstorms and dirty potatoes gathering mildew in a sack that emanated a foul stench. But the potatoes had been somewhere else he'd lived. Or maybe nowhere at all. He'd had the superstition since childhood that he would die by electrocution, and he did remember that at least part of the fear was founded by the one unfortunate incident in his boyhood during which he reached for a light switch that was illicitly and insufficiently wired to a washing machine in a neighbor's flat, and the current that flowed from the open circuit through his body in an irregular pattern felt like sharp cogs grinding his insides, causing extreme pain, but also making him itch badly.

For Damian Meier, elementary education, up to the fourth year, took the usual route of every developing student in the system, that is: nothing spectacular or indicating any early inclination of mastery in a discipline either way. In the fifth year, Damian Meier was felled by Mathematics, in particular quadratic equations and the circumference of objects, and was promptly told by an elderly despotic instructor with flabby underarms and the propensity to use the edge of a ruler on pupils' knuckles that, although he would never pass the baccalaureate exam in a few years, he would make an efficient ditch-digger in the army.

The Private First Class designation that Damian Meier received in the army after he, indeed, proved he could not pass the baccalaureate exam but instead did make an efficient ditch-digger was the first time he was bestowed anything with the words "First" in the title, and he looked upon the status with great pride. Not long after showing various sergeants (and sometimes even colonels who liked to inspect such unimportant things) that he could excavate an outhouse hole within a few hours with no help, Damian Meier was moved to the motor pool as an assistant mechanic in charge of keeping full the diesel supply, properly working sparkplugs, and updating inventory in a notebook. Accounting, it seems, was also a strong skill of Damian Meier's, despite his failed academic career. There was no need to find the area of circular objects in accounting, only keep track of their numbers.

From time to time, he would send crates of grapes and homemade plum brandy to a vague address in the capital where he was somewhat unsure that his mother and father resided. The goods were never returned to his post, thus leaving Damian Meier satisfied he was executing his filial duties despite the absence of any communication or a simple word of thanks from the parents at the address.

The revolution began at Easter and spread from the northwest of the country quickly. As with nearly every revolution, massive protests by dissatisfied university undergraduates swelled in city plazas, demanding the resignation of the president and his government and instituting free elections. As with every revolution, the government mobilized not just the army, but also a large, expeditionary force of miners and other workers and armed them with batons in order that they be set upon the demonstrators, indicating that the working class was not to be upended by intellectuals with obtuse ideals and eyeglasses.

Damian Meier was not one of those assigned by the government to play the role of a miner or a worker. He was already a trained soldier (Private First Class), and his skills were better exploited firing a rifle into the soft flesh covering the cranium of a dissenter, not swinging a club in the manner of a corrupt Cro-Magnon. Bureaucracy decreed that Damian Meier could be more effective in his efforts to stifle the revolution from a long distance, for example as a sniper in an empty room with the windows removed high up in a housing tenement overlooking the goings-on, thus conserving energy as well as time. But bureaucracy was trumped by higher-up bureaucracy with a different goal.

The colonel who explained the strange assignment was bony and tall with pink skin and had an unusual name like Haas or Foos. It wasn't ultimately important to Damian Meier, who imagined there was a double letter in the surname and then simply forgot about it. The officer was adamant about the importance of the mission and often, as he was explaining the rudiments at a much closer distance to his face than Damian Meier was comfortable with, he slapped his own arms as if he were squashing mosquitoes. During the briefing, Damian Meier felt he was going to pull out his knife and cut off the colonel's earlobe for no reason. He was surprised by how unmoved he felt thinking about the colonel's sudden misfortune. After all, they were attempting to quell a revolution and many different inequities occurred within the context of such conflicts; a missing earlobe would not invite inquiries. No one pushed too hard to extract responsibility for anything during trying times.

The street that Damian Meier was assigned to guard by colonel Haas or Foos divided the city almost exactly in half. It was comprised of large, black cobblestones that had been quarried nearly six hundred years before by Ottoman Empire slaves (*kuls*) and brought to the city on the backs of donkeys and the *kuls* themselves. The crux of the assignment was simple: the street was to be held and kept at all costs by the forces of the government. Damian Meier did not ask why. One, because a Private First Class in the army never questioned orders given by a colonel, and two, because he assumed a thoroughfare that divides in half a city under siege must be of great strategic importance to one side or another.

The first twelve hours at the post were passed in a strange kind of guarded boredom for Damian Meier. From both sides surrounding the street he could hear clearly that bullets belonging to the army were being answered with Molotov cocktails and other homemade incendiary devices thrown by the revolutionaries in a kind of turbulent, aggressive argument. The bullets, he assumed, were more accurate in their intent and thus winning the quarrel.

A ghastly howl, that of a woman's, reverberated through his territory at one point. It bounced off the cobblestones and around the centuries-old edifices that had been hastily abandoned at the time the unrest came to the city. The screams exited out like knives above the roofs and swirled in with clouds of blue and black smoke floating above. Damian Meier was aware that a woman was being raped before her probable slaughter, likely by several army soldiers. Despite his allegiance to the government forces, at that moment he felt he could turn on his violating comrades and execute murder, but not to exact justice for the woman. For another reason, which he couldn't explain. Instead, he just watched the clouds of smoke from the nearby fighting and burning assemble themselves into weird shapes above his street: human limbs, a sausage, cauliflower, alien submarines.

But Damian Meier had an assignment. Atrocities, discrimination, partisanship, bias, prejudice, and genocide were all interrelated components of the maelstrom that aimed to topple that comfortable permanence in the world of governments and hierarchy. The street, colonel Haas or Foos decreed, must be held and the post never abandoned.

Fighting stretched into the night but never once were the boundaries of the street breached by anyone, as if an alliance had been formed by the warring sides to designate the thoroughfare a demilitarized zone, one which Damian Meier was to protect and maintain. This baffled him and enraged him. And so he remained somewhat pointlessly in his guardhouse at attention with the rifle loaded and extra magazines filling a large bucket at his feet. From time to time a Molotov cocktail or makeshift incendiary weapon would be hurled from one side to the other, safely passing through the airspace of the street, never landing in it. Through the screaming and cursing from both sides, Damian Meier dreamed of rolling a cigarette with good tobacco from another country and longing to take part in the conflict.

At dawn the sun burned through the stench of charred bodies and smoke, and a somewhat drowsy Damian Meier wished very much he could shoot someone. He put his hand on the holster of his pistol and although he didn't draw it, this calmed him.

The army must have moved equipment and artillery overnight, because right at the time a person would be taking a coffee, dissolving the cobwebs of a difficult slumber, Damian Meier counted six consecutive shells flying supersonically above his street heading toward the other side. The projectiles screamed oddly, like pigs being slaughtered with hunting knives. The concussion of the shells landing a short distance away knocked his cup of cold cabbage soup into the bucket of bullets, and the murderous rage inside Damian Meier's guts grew at this simple injustice. He decided that he was going to stab the colonel with his bayonet the next time the officer came.

Four days after he was assigned to guard the street, Damian Meier longed for things in school to have turned out differently. He wished he understood quadratic equations. He wished he passed the baccalaureate. He coveted time at a university without realizing the laborious, rigorous curricula. Had he gone on to higher education, his allegiance would likely have belonged with the revolutionaries, and he would have been throwing Molotov cocktails instead of guarding an empty street that was conspicuously not important enough to be taken by either side. His life would not have been futile. It would have ended at the gallows resolved and complete.

Inside his guardhouse he sliced off a circular piece of head cheese and attempted to solve its radius using $2(\pi)r = c$, but he could not. Instead, he longed for mustard.

In order to coax the fighting into spilling across his street and thus plunge him into the conflict, Damian Meier started fires, whistled, screamed, and marched incessantly up and down, stomping his boots on the cobblestones so violently that he nearly dislocated one of his knees.

On the sixth night the fighting around him suddenly ceased. Not one sound came from the warring parties. The noise of revolution was instead replaced by chirping birds, a melodious singing that reverberated throughout the entire street, bouncing off the buildings in a continuous, reflected pattern that multiplied over itself until a cacophony of music enveloped the entire space. Perplexed, Damian Meier left his post and walked to the middle of the thoroughfare. At that moment he knew he was going to swallow a bullet that would enter through his jaw and lodge itself in the back of the throat. In his larynx, he felt the strange tickle of grinding electrical current he had once experienced as a boy, as if the cylindrical projectile generated its own power. And then, in the midst of incessant birdsong he began to scream obscure phrases and dubious mathematical formulas, all the while wishing he would grow taller.

The intruder came suddenly from behind the guardhouse, nearly seventy meters away. It was clueless, walking without purpose toward Damian Meier who quickly raised his weapon to the shoulder and aimed. Not noticing the impending doom or even smelling Damian Meier's acrid odor from having stood guard and not washed in nearly a week, the trespasser turned his head sideways momentarily, pricking his ears at a peculiar sweeping sound coming from an alley perpendicular to the street. Could someone, a cleaning woman who had stayed behind from some sort of obtuse allegiance, actually be scouring the front steps of her home with a broom? Damian Meier shot. It was clean and acceptable: into the head through the right eye. The *pop* of the rifle funneled out vertically with a short echo.

The animal was thrown back from the violence discharged to its skull. And then it collapsed like a deflated set of bagpipes, making a slight gasp-like sound from the oxygen forced out of its mouth.

It was a muscular dog, maybe a husky, but an old dog who had strayed. Damian Meier thought he had grey wolf in him. He walked up to the animal and placed his boot on the dog's neck, pressing hard. Blood squeezed out of his mouth and gathered in a puddle first, before slowly flooding into the channels of the cobblestones and advancing toward an undefined destination. In his left eye, the one organ that was not mutilated by the bullet, the dog had formed a tear but the secretion had not yet had the chance to flow down, and so it gathered into a miniature pool in the conjunctiva.

Damian Meier did not notice it.

★

At the awards ceremony, the Colonel-General who pinned the medal for courageous combat service on Damian Meier's left breast leaned in and whispered: The line between not killing and killing is quite faint . . . almost indistinguishable. That is what you are receiving this medal for. The officer's breath smelled of onions and bile. In fact, the officer said, killing nowadays doesn't even require a weapon, only a pen. That is also why you are receiving this medal. From here on, you'll merely be required to use a pen—a much simpler assignment, don't you agree? And much more civilized.

Official pictures were taken of the recipients. They stood erect—proud men adorned by golden epaulets like sticks in mud wrapped with sparkling garlands. In time, these photos would be altered accordingly to stay consistent with the People's dictated changes in the historical events of the particular day. A revolution thwarted always carried with it purges. Purges were a natural consequence of change or fickle orders given by men with pockmarked faces from offices with plush carpeting. Damian Meier would come to understand this not long after the medal was pinned to his uniform and subsequently given an office in the Central Committee building presiding over Revolution Plaza and becoming part of the bureaucracy of the People.

★

There were two telephones on his desk. The one with the red receiver had no dial or any means whatsoever of redirecting the line away from the permanent destination to which it was connected: the secret security force that served as the information as well as punitive organ of the People. During the three years that Damian Meier worked in the spacious, brightly lit Victorian room surveilling Revolution Plaza, he never once received communication on or had to dispatch orders using the red receiver. But the telephone was always there, looming. Finality rested on his desk every day with a blank, nonplussed demeanor. It concerned itself with the personal affairs of every functionary. The red telephone was where and how everything ended for everyone.

Ivanov walked into the room with a manila folder under his arm. He placed it on Damian Meier's desk and quickly passed a look over the red receiver. To what? To make sure all was well? To look for a secret signal? Ivanov was a survivor from the previous revolution. He was the rat living inside the pipes that swam to the air pocket whenever the conduits were flooded. Damian Meier knew that from the day Ivanov was assigned to him. There were men like Ivanov who outlasted everything: revolutions, death, history. These men were bridges reaching backwards and forward in ideology. They allowed for everything to happen or not happen, including time. Men like Ivanov were always assigned to men like

Damian Meier and most always severely outranked their assignees. Ivanov was probably a general.

Do you have a working pen, Ivanov asked. He wore a brown suit that was frayed at the cuffs of the trousers and jacket sleeves. He stank of sweat and kitchen. It was hard to see down to the ruthlessness of the man through his modest clothes. The suit evoked pity and charity not terror. It was a disorienting layer of humanity that, on Ivanov's part, was either intended or accidental. Damian Meier patted himself and looked at the man's veins pulsating on top of his hands. Ivanov left a writing instrument next to the folder and made a strange gesture. Damian Meier thought he heard Ivanov's heels click and expected a bow. But the man merely tapped on the paperwork inside the folder. By two o'clock, he said. And then he let himself out.

From the window, Damian Meier had a clear look at the row of old mulberry trees delineating the edge of the asphalt pedestrian path that undulated around the plaza and flowed out along Boulevard Magyar. A functionary, an ordinary looking man with a shameful piece of hand luggage used as a briefcase, crossed the plaza and walked perpendicularly across the path into the shadow of the mulberry trees. Damian Meier craned his neck but the glass prevented him from switching to a good angle. The man could only be seen from the chest down now, his half torso swallowed by the tree and its shadows. The pitiful briefcase was dropped to the ground. Both his arms thrust up into the lower crown folds of the fruit tree, shaking the branches. It was a curious scene and Damian Meier expected to see a policeman at the location immediately, investigating and making an arrest for defacing public space. A few pedestrians walked by, all of whom purposefully fixed their eyes away from the infraction the functionary was committing. How curious, Damian Meier thought. The man is cutting down branches, surely. But with what? He hadn't noticed any type of saw or tool. He must be ripping the tree limbs with his own hands. Why?

When the man finished his deed, he picked up the briefcase and emerged from the shadow, chewing. His trouser pockets as well as the small pouch on the left breast of his shirt bulged with what Damian Meier assumed were the tree's fruit. The functionary looked across the plaza quickly, scanning the area as if hoping to spot a waiting accomplice. Then he wiped his lips clean of trickling juice with his sleeve and took the pedestrian path out toward Boulevard Magyar. Across from the tree which had been violated, standing firmly in the plaza in front of the bronze statue of Michael the Brave, a student pioneer—a child of no more than nine years—took out a small, inadequately bound notepad and wrote forcefully and frenetically the infraction by the hungry functionary that she had witnessed.

The People aren't interested in individual cases, Ivanov said. His voice sent a twitch to the left cheek of Damian Meier.

It was a sharp stab with the blade of a pen knife, a direct, violent strike that reached in a short line deep into the muscle of the face. Ivanov had stealthily come back with more paperwork. How long had he been standing there? Could he have seen what Damian Meier had spied outside? Was he addressing the infraction of that poor functionary who merely helped himself to a few handfuls of the People's fruit? No, the People are not interested in names on a list, comrade, Ivanov said. What's more important in our situation is that the names themselves realize that retaliation has been triggered and that the earthquake has arrived under their feet. The People understand that. They are in accord with that, Ivanov said. He placed the bulging manila folder on the desk next to the other paperwork. And these by three o'clock, comrade, he said.

Damian Meier sat at the desk and slid over the first pile of paperwork. He looked briefly through the first dozen pages. They were the usual confessions extracted by security agents in the basement, four floors below his office: violation of the People's discipline, enemy of the People who sows discord into society, intent to conspire against the People, conduct immoral to the well-being of the People, treason against the People. Very few confessions listed any more details. The ones that did were such outrageous tales that, instead of preposterous and comical, they became chilling.

The documents were written in longhand by the confessors themselves. Damian Meier's duty was to transcribe and sign them, making them official documents by stamping the People's insignia in the lower left-hand corner of the paper. He rolled in a segment of carbon sandwiched by two blank sheets into the .Xo typewriter issued and registered specifically to him by the Office of Information and Communications. The machine worked well. Its only flaw was the non-functioning letter "I," an annoying situation which Damian Meier always circumvented by substituting the letter with the number "1."

At two o'clock, Ivanov entered the office and removed the typewritten, signed, and stamped paperwork brought in earlier. He asked Damian Meier if he needed anything and announced he would come back in an hour.

You should take part in the morning exercises, Ivanov said and pushed the cup and saucer toward Damian Meier. The tea was weak, probably strained a fourth or fifth time through the filter. It would help with your precarious condition, Ivanov smiled. Damian Meier held his left hand. The last three fingers had been numb for several months, a condition he attributed to excessive typing and relentless use of longhand, signing not just the daily quota of confessions but dozens of additional permits and decrees in the name of the People. But, as Ivanov removed the second folder with official paperwork from his desk, Damian Meier realized he hadn't mentioned his affliction to anyone. Ivanov tapped the file with his fingers, turned, and quietly shut the door behind him.

Damian Meier remained standing. What did Ivanov mean, precarious? What was precarious about his numb fingers, if he even knew about them? And which condition? The numbness? His own private convictions about the People? Ivanov was an intelligent rat. He would never just be making idle conversation. Certainly another office kept track of who took part in recreational activities. There was always another typewriter, a signature, and a stamp on paperwork.

Damian Meier sat and clicked the pen. With its point he pressed into the bottom fleshy area of the ring finger on his left hand. He felt nothing. And then he decided that next morning he was going to join the others in the half hour of arm circles, jumping jacks, and stretching out in the yard. Ivanov was right. The People were right; all he needed was consistent exercise.

★

The flat issued to him was not small; it was comprised of two medium-sized rooms, a modest bathroom with enough space for tub, sink, and toilet, and a separate kitchen—the largest room in the dwelling. The previous tenant must have had a child; there was a wire mesh rigged on the outside of the kitchen window, presumably to keep the child from falling nine stories down to the alley that delineated the shorter side of the rectangular, concrete apartment building.

Damian Meier hung his coat on the hook in the vestibule. He took off his shoes and slid them neatly under the modest side table against the wall. He placed his key on the table, underneath his handkerchief, and walked to the washroom where he urinated while sitting on the porcelain vessel. At that moment, a wave of hatred slammed across his chest and he wished Ivanov to be purged. With the flush of the toilet he could be sent back to the sewer pipes, from where he came.

In the kitchen, Damian Meier had a yoghurt for dinner and listened to the gargantuan People-issued radio until its tubes began to overheat and pop, finally drowning out the banal analytical program. He stood, looked up, tracing the strange geometric corners of the walls up to the ceiling, hoping to spot something. And then he heated water in the pot on the kitchen stove. He filled the tub a third of the way, enough to cover his thighs when he sat in it, and then he climbed in.

The telephone in the vestibule buzzed. From the tub, Damian Meier counted thirty-six rings before it fell silent again. On the other end of the line, the case officer assigned to debrief Damian Meier was aware of his presence in the flat and would call back in ten minutes. An excuse would have to be given: a severely upset stomach that required more time spent in the washroom than the average. The unpleasant condition would be attributed to the spoiled state of the yoghurt eaten for dinner earlier. Everything connected safely and logically.

The case officer identified himself by his last name and a number. It was always the same name and number, but every new conversation had to be documented for the Office of Information and Communications. The monthly debriefing usually lasted no longer than fifteen minutes and included standard questions about work productivity and personal details regarding every aspect of daily life. When asked about missing the call ten minutes earlier, Damian Meier told the officer on the other end of the crackling, tapped line about his stomach misfortune. Immediately he thought it wise to leave the yoghurt jar unwashed on the kitchen table for the agents who would enter his flat the next day in order to search for evidence corroborating the story.

What of the woman in 8A who beats her rugs free of dust in the courtyard alongside the other widow in 8C? the case officer asked Damian Meier. Are they speaking to one another under the loud cover of their chores? Damian Meier reported that he hadn't seen either of them talking. But they are out there together, always, the case officer said. They must be saying something to one another. There is always a reason two comrades are consistently together. And that reason isn't to be silent. Would you disagree? said the case officer. The line crackled when Damian Meier spoke.

★

Ivanov came in with paperwork. These by four, and these by tomorrow afternoon or sooner, he said. Better sooner. This pile has been typed already and contains approvals of permits for building walls. Take care how you sign comrade, because space is severely limited and the sheets are thin. If you press too hard, the ink will go through. Damian Meier's handwritten signature was elaborate and pompous, Ivanov thought. It was the fancy inscription of a man holding vanity inside, or secret dreams. It was the signature of an artist not a worker or a functionary of the People.

He pushed the paperwork across the desk toward the typewriter without taking his eyes off Damian Meier who was staring at the red telephone, his face contorted. All is well, comrade? Ivanov asked. It looks like you are guarding the line. Are you expecting something? Damian Meier offered an excuse for his aloofness, citing the upset stomach he mentioned to his case officer on the telephone the week before. Many others can perform when even under the greatest discomfort or stress, Ivanov said patronizingly. He tugged at a fingernail, trying to dislodge something from underneath. Those are the virtues of the People. Would you disagree, comrade?

In the early evening, Damian Meier walked across Revolution Plaza toward the mulberry trees, tracing the steps of the interloper he had seen from his office window. The swollen fruit hung from the branches begging to be collected.

85

A great amount had fallen on the path just below the corona of the trees and had been squashed under the feet of passers-by. The deep-red and purple fruit left stains on the asphalt that resembled dried pools of blood, as if a massive amount of people had been executed underneath the trees, their bodies removed. Damian Meier paused and looked around for informers. No one he could observe was idling and watching. There were no pioneers or students with notepads lurking around the statue of Michael the Brave. He doubled back toward the Central Committee building, walked around the massive edifice, and headed out on the People's Boulevard toward his flat.

In the kitchen, he listened to the radio program while he ate potato soup and two thick slices of bread. And then he scooped cottage cheese into a bowl on top of which he placed a dollop of sour cream. There was no water running this day, so he placed the dishes into the sink and walked to the washroom to urinate.

Before he retired, Damian Meier quietly walked down one floor in bare feet. He approached 8A and put his ear on the door. He could hear nothing. He listened for quite some time until the cables of the elevator suddenly groaned, pulling up the weight of the car. The lift stopped short of the eighth floor and deposited its cargo below. Metal doors slammed and the cables again strained to lower the car to the ground floor.

Damian Meier's next intention was to walk softly across to 8C and listen in, but when he turned toward the door he noticed that there was a slight change in the level of light coming through the peephole, a quick flicker. There was quiet movement in the flat. Someone in 8C had been watching him.

That night Damian Meier dressed himself fully, put on his shoes, packed a small suitcase with a change of underclothes and a half piece of soap, and then went to bed. Lying on his back trying to fall asleep, he thought about adding a toothbrush to his bag but decided against it. After the debriefing and interrogation that he expected, he would likely not have teeth left.

★

They didn't come for him like they came for most others. They afforded him the prestige of his position within the People's party and took into account his loyal service in the army during the quelling of the revolution so many years ago. Damian Meier had underestimated his worth. He didn't have to sleep in his shoes, fully dressed, and packed for those seven months.

When the time for his arrest came, his handler showed up at a civilized time in the evening after supper. Even the intensity of the knock at the door carried with it a certain amount of melancholy and respect. The rap was that of a friend coming to pay a social visit, not of a security agent serving an order for arrest.

Damian Meier opened the door and stepped aside so that the man could walk unmolested into the small vestibule. You may hang your scarf on the hook, Damian Meier said. The man raised his hand and declined. Would you like some tea first? I have fresh bags, Damian Meier said and lifted his chin toward the kitchen. That would be fine comrade, Ivanov said. He let Damian Meier walk ahead.

We're lucky this evening we have water. Tuesdays, Thursdays, and Sundays this section of the building is allowed running water. Yes, quite fortunate, Ivanov said. And by the luck of the draw, as well: water on Sundays, no less. What a great luxury. May I assume you'll have sugar in your tea? Ivanov nodded: always grateful to feel warm during these frigid days. Ivanov realized how strange his declaration for desire of comfort might have sounded to the man who was being arrested and who would soon know none of that.

Damian Meier dropped two cubes into both cups and slowly poured boiling water over the small pouches. This would be the last time for tea. He took care to pour water a little slower. He took care to observe the change in water color from the infusion of the tea bag. Everything became more vivid and purposeful, even the nonessential details of the moment, like making tea. Like the minute bounce of the sugar cube against the porcelain bottom of the cup. Like the intermittent *ding* of the teaspoon as it stirs.

I have a radio if you wish to hear something, Damian Meier said. It just needs a minute for the tubes to warm up. We shouldn't be too long, comrade, Ivanov said. He sipped carefully, taking care not to burn his lips and tongue. I asked for special concessions on the timeframe because of your esteemed position comrade, but we shouldn't take advantage. Of course not, Damian Meier said. He slurped the tea from his cup with urgency. The men sat in silence for a few minutes. Outside it had started to rain ice pellets, and the wind sometimes drove them obliquely, almost horizontally, into the kitchen window like tiny fingers rapping on the glass desiring to be let in from the misery.

Was it the widow in 8C that betrayed me? Damian Meier asked. Or 8A? Ivanov gently placed his tea on the saucer. My darling comrade, we all betray our own selves eventually. There is no need for anyone else to do the deed. We are all made in the same way. We are born predisposed like that. Consider it a failsafe within the heart of all comrades. And when that time comes . . . when we cannot be useful in any other way because of all of that rotting and spoiling inside of us, the People are owed a fresh change. Wouldn't you agree? The old, cancerous dog must not be let to suffer. He must be shot. You comrade, of all people, know that to be truer than true. You have been part of it. You have seen that first hand.

But the People aren't interested in individual cases, Damian Meier said and watched his handler's face closely. Ivanov knew Damian Meier wasn't afraid or stalling for time. There was no time anyway. Ivanov knew that the question was meant to expose the weakness of hypocrisy and flaws of the People. He knew that Damian Meier was attempting to assert a position of individuality and freedom within, in these final minutes. The question was meant for Damian Meier himself. He was moving toward clarity and Ivanov knew it. But you see, comrade, you are not an individual case, Ivanov said. If you think of yourself as that, you are a failure and have been rotten from the very beginning and you should have been hanged long ago. You have never been an individual case, comrade. Not even from before you were born. Not even from when you didn't exist.

The men finished their tea. Ivanov stood and walked to the window. He looked down at the van waiting. The driver had opened the window and was smoking, despite the weather. Ivanov looked at his elbow resting on the door frame. We shouldn't be too long, comrade. Of course, Damian Meier said. They stepped out into the hallway and called up the elevator. Damian Meier left the flat door unlocked for the next tenant. The elevator cables moaned under their weight when they entered the tight cabin, and Damian Meier had a brief strange feeling in his stomach of plunging down nine floors. It was going to be easy, all of it.

The first two floors of Damian Meier's apartment building were occupied by the offices of an Agro-Tourism branch of the Interior Department. Here, the walls came within centimeters of the elevator car moving up or down. There weren't any residential hallways, just the plain brown walls that had always made Damian Meier feel as if he was locked alive in a coffin. Slowly descending now, staring through the thin rectangular glass slats of the elevator, Ivanov's eyes caught suddenly the crude, strange type of graffiti that had been carved by a blade or a screwdriver into the otherwise bare wall: *Isus Hristos*.

In your heart, Ivanov said, you know that this is best for the People. There can only be this way, and you know truly that this is best. Do you trust the judgment of the People to do what's best for them, comrade? Do you trust that this has to be?

Yes, Damian Meier said. I do.

INTERVIEW WITH JUAN WEIDER
(Published in Nonbinary Review-Alphanumeric, 2016)

WHEN JUAN WEIDER disappeared in December of 1989, a small group of his admirers began to tell stories manufactured from their own dreams or nightmares. The legends varied greatly and some were truly outrageous, like most stories about cruel characters or emperors usually are. But the one most accepted by Weider's strange circle of fans (if that's what those kinds of people can be called), wannabes, and even the few living relatives of victims he'd left scattered in his wake unintentionally, was that he'd gone into the northeastern Andean highlands of Ecuador to record (for himself or posterity) the precise time each morning the day's first bird sang.

This story came replete with details such as: Juan Weider kept intricately detailed notebooks of the type genus of bird first to vocalize and highly accurate songbird times (to the millisecond, the idea was that he had a digital stopwatch, of course) written in ink made from particles of carbon black, shipped by mule from Quito to his one-room shack in the jungle. And: the only man authorized to deliver these types of shipments was of Chachi heritage who only spoke Cha'palaa—the Barbacoan language of his ancestors. Like the missionary P. Alberto Vittadello who had lived for seven years among the Chachi tribe, Juan Weider had fully immersed himself in the Amazon jungle of north Ecuador.

Juan Weider was an interrogator and a writer. Many thought he was brother of the Chilean skywriting poet *cum* legend Carlos, who had the same last name, served as executioner for the Pinochet regime, and who also disappeared in 1989, just before Pinochet stepped down. But he wasn't. In fact, Juan Weider may have been a woman. His name may have been Ivana, according to some who worked with him (dull tasks such as stamping documents and paperwork and performed other menial administrative duties). If he wasn't a woman after all, then some of his victims may have known him as inquisitor Ivanov. One thing's for sure, if any of them ever answered to a certain Ivanov during their interrogations before they signed confessions, none would be alive to corroborate the name. Perhaps those rumors were born out of nightmares.

When Juan Weider wasn't interrogating or torturing people in the basements of non-descript Eastern European government buildings, he was writing and publishing Samizdats filled with fiction criticizing the morals of high-level government officials—the same ones that employed his services. Yes, he would change names, but everyone knew that for example Ivan was Ivor, minister of security who liked to float in his large private bathhouse and have little boys suckling on his toes (like Caligula), Roxana was Ruxandra, wife of the interior minister who forced her lovers to walk on all fours, meowing like cats or whimpering like injured dogs, and so forth. The Samizdats circulated underground among various intellectuals and artists, and Juan Weider became a legend on par with the famous broadcaster from (banned) Radio Free Europe, Sebastian Blackbeard. During those days, Juan Weider wrote under the pseudonym Jean-Francois Ian.

Over the years, Juan Weider interrogated many of the same intellectuals and artists that were enamored of his illicit writing, most of whom (if not all) paying with their lives. None of them knew that he was Jean-Francois Ian, responsible for the same material that they were accused of possessing, reading, and propagating.

Before he disappeared in December 1989, Jean-Francois Ian published an interview with Juan Weider. The piece (which was in reality a self-interview) was a shattering exposé of the interrogation and information extraction business that all governments (not just repressive regimes) conduct. It is because of this interview that some believe Juan Weider was a woman. No man could speak with such sensitivity and elegance, such complex sensibility and humanity about the psychological methods of interrogation, extracting (false) confessions, and torture of citizens as Juan Weider did in his interview with Jean-Francois Ian. Weider spoke of empathy. It was vital that a high degree of empathy exist within the interrogator for his subject. In fact, Weider said, the more sensitive an individual, the sterner and more effective an interrogator he would make. And later even an official executioner, but that was a different position altogether that required a different set of sensibilities, skills, and a melancholic sense of history. This is why artists are perfect for this job, Weider said in his interview. Artists are the best at torturing people. Especially other artists. (Of course, themselves, as well.) It is in light of ideas such as this that some readers believed Juan Weider was a woman.

It is interesting that Juan Weider chose to walk into the Ecuadorian rainforest, the home to many fleeing Nazis after WWII. But perhaps with a name like that, Juan Weider's decision was wise. The most efficient way to disappear is to simply live among other monsters like yourself. No one cares to notice. It's as if everyone is living before a mirror. No one wants to see their own reflection. Certainly not anyone in the business that Juan Weider had been in: torture and writing.

It is also interesting why Juan Weider chose to disappear at all that late December 1989. It is true that the Wall had crumbled in Europe, and young idealists began to take it apart with hammers, screwdrivers, even sickles (ironically), but Weider had not been anyone important. He was just a usual functioning part in a terrifyingly voracious machine. Historically, he wasn't on any kind of radar. At least he wasn't anyone important enough to be stood in a courtyard, given a blindfold, and shot.

In fact, most of those deemed important enough usually to be executed during a regime change, the ones in charge of the oppression and inequities, switched sides. Or, rather even more simply, switched labels. Now they were democratic or liberal or leftist or green. Some of these people were bold or egotistical, and they announced their allegiance to the natural, conservative movement, banking on people's sense of melancholy: remember how good it was when . . . But in the end they all made money, and more importantly they all retained power. The heads that rolled after the Wall came down continued to be of those that were never complicit in the dealings of government.

Juan Weider's father stayed put for a while. He was an old dog, though not subtle or intelligent in the way one thinks of intelligence. He played on people's vanity and charity, switching masterfully between the two as he needed. But all old dogs know the streets; they can tell which way things are going to go just from smelling the piss on the sidewalks or light poles.

After Juan Weider disappeared, his father went on to denounce him publicly (playing on the vanity of the Social Democratic Party, the group that grabbed power first after the revolution). He dedicated himself to freedom and people's rights, although by that time he was an old man about to draw a pension from the state and had no usable skills to contribute to society—he had been a mediocre actor with a small theater company that never travelled outside the country but was known for putting on plays by Michel de Ghelderode.

In his days of retirement, the old man undertook a project that he thought would revolutionize not just the world of theater but that of art in general: he began to re-write de Ghelderode's play *Christophe Colomb*. In the old man's version, the explorer becomes addicted to visions of Saint Anthony in the New World due to his use of peyote and disappears among American Indians, never to return to Spain with the claimed land. The New World remains unknown, diseases are not introduced, and empires like the Inca go on to thrive for a few hundred years before they effectively destroy one another in war and genocide. (Like I said, he had no usable skills to contribute to society.)

In 1999, on the brink of a new millennium, Juan Weider's father left for Germany. In the small town of Aachen (sometimes in English the city is referred to as Aix-la-Chapelle), he befriended a woman, an émigré hailing from the same area of the country in which he was born, although she was fifteen years younger. No one who knew them (there were very few) could say what they had in common. They barely spoke to one another in public. The woman was an invalid for some reason (he never cared to find out why), confined to a wheelchair and living with her mother in a small but conveniently located flat in the spa town.

The home was a small jewel, replete with all the necessary amenities and perks that the town offered. For example, Juan Weider's father could walk to the city square leisurely and take his Turkish coffee at any of the several cafés or browse books by obscure Slavic authors at his favorite used bookstore one block from the flat. If he wished, he could take a train into Brussels for that big city feeling some people yearn after, though provincial as he was, Juan Weider's father never did. The train station, anyway, was a ten-minute walk from the flat.

The apartment belonged to the émigré's elderly mother, and the arrangement between Juan Weider's father and his woman in the wheelchair seemed to be this: he took care of the infirm woman and her mother, and when the mother died (which was to be soon, based upon her age and fragility), Juan

Weider was to inherit the flat. But, as with everything in life, well-laid plans never materialize.

Juan Weider's father met Niko by mistake. One damp and cold autumn afternoon, he took the wrong streetcar to a festival the town council was sponsoring in celebration of Oktoberfest. It was quite some time before Juan Weider's father realized his mistake, as he had been lost for a while in his thoughts about the entire business of inheriting the flat. The invalid's mother had not shown any signs of demise whatsoever, in fact just the opposite. It seemed as if a revival had occurred. She had taken to going out for hours-long walks by herself daily and even began to appreciate Wagner and Mahler with her afternoon cup of tea—a sure sign of longevity—for music most certainly adds years to a life. The woman was stronger than ever, and Juan Weider's father was trapped now taking care of an invalid and her youthful mother who seemed to be living life in reverse.

Niko was an émigré from Sofia, Bulgaria. He had arrived in Aachen via sponsorship from a local Lutheran church. The church prided itself in doing God's charity work by helping destitute political émigrés. Once arrived, those sponsored were offered food and lodging within the church's confines, as well as some vocational training, language lessons, and a small stipend until the sods were mostly integrated into German society and let loose upon the world. In return, the refugees had to commit two evenings and every Sunday each week to service for the church.

It's all bullshit, Niko told Juan Weider's father on the wrong streetcar. But you know how that is. Yes, Juan Weider's father said. You do what you have to do in order to eat. Before they parted ways, the two men agreed to form a partnership in an import/retail business of rabbit pelts. The idea seems odd, true, but given the latitude and harsh autumn and winter weather of their new country, Niko's plan wasn't at all bad. Through his connections in provincial Bulgaria, Niko would be able to procure for half the price of his stipend an egregious amount of rabbit pelts. The fur would then be used to manufacture warm hats, much like those worn by Russians in Siberia, and sold to the Germans. Juan Weider's father, not having any prospects in life other than an invalid and her youthful mother, agreed to provide initially 500 DM ($1,000) for start-up costs and purchases of pelts, then a monthly sum of 100 DM commensurate with how fast (or slow) the business would grow.

After they shook hands like two old gentlemen having just engaged in a gentleman's agreement, and Juan Weider's father stepped off the streetcar, a euphoric feeling came over the old man. It was a feeling of validation and entitlement. He rushed to his flat among the mist and cold full of verve and vitality. He did not wait for the lift. Instead, he walked up the four stories two stairs at a time, not at all feeling the strain.

Inside, the invalid's mother had fallen asleep in her room watching a television program. The door was shut but the volume reverberated throughout the entire apartment. Juan Weider's father felt the tide rising inside of him like honey. It was vicious, but it carried sweetness along with it. And after all, the old man now had a purpose and was going to make a name for himself within the town's community.

In one brusque and resolute movement, he grabbed hold of the woman's wheelchair at its handles, navigated the corners out of her room and around into the hallway, and picking up force and speed, headed for the door of the flat, which he had not bothered to close upon coming in. The woman first inquired confused then quickly protested as it seemed Juan Weider's father was not intent on stopping short of the door. By the time they went through and into the hallway of the building, the old man was nearly running. With one satisfying, swift motion, he heaved the chair together with the woman down the stairs. The invalid toppled forward and immediately broke her neck (Juan Weider's father heard the snap—it was like breaking a putrid, rotten twig), with the chair following closely and finally landing on her dislocated body, together the mess of bones and metal resting on the landing below.

Mutti, Liebling. I'm finished, *der Schatz.* The old man yelled back into the flat, but the invalid's mother said nothing. Nothing could be heard over the volume of the television program. Juan Weider's father shut the door to the flat and called up the lift from the lobby.

Unlike the old man, Juan Weider's mother chose to stay and live what turned out to be an unremarkable life in the same apartment in which her son had been born. Having been divorced from Juan Weider's father for quite a long time (Juan Weider was ten years of age when the court proceedings officially recognized the split), the woman finally decided to go back to her maiden name: Rossetti.

In reality, her father's name had been Rossettus—he was a Macedonian with Lebanese heritage—but as World War I broke out all over Europe, his family thought it unwise to keep a name associated with the Great Powers (the Ottoman Empire), so they changed it to the more Italian-sounding Rossetti when he was sixteen years of age. It was, in retrospect, the right idea. Two years later, the Italians along with the Allies prevailed.

Juan Weider's mother, Rossetti, began and finished her career at AutoTractor, a company that would be bought eventually by Eicher, a West German manufacturer of agricultural machines, located near Munich. After the Wall came down in 1989 and Juan Weider disappeared, Rossetti welcomed the new change in ownership and management style. She found the Germans distant and efficient. She liked the intensity of the foreigners, and she especially enjoyed the punctuality with which monthly accounting meetings were held.

Rossetti often lulled herself to sleep at night imagining what she would do when she could travel to Bavaria to tour the facilities of her new employer. She dreamed of creamy desserts, of having coffee with a Berliner or slices of Buchtein. She dreamed of Black Forest Cake and Blachindla and Dampfnudel.

But Rossetti never travelled to Munich. Instead, she walked along side of Lake Herastrau every evening after work and often opted to buy her small supper in take-away containers from the restaurant across from her flat. The establishment sold brown beer in bottles with twist-off caps—something that made Rossetti very happy for some reason that she couldn't name. (It's not as if she didn't own a bottle opener.) To compensate for her lack of travel to Germany, she would often take-away two small, thin slices of schnitzel, which she would eat with mustard in front of the television in the evenings and wash down with Dortmunder Union beer.

Seven years after Juan Weider disappeared into the jungle of Ecuador, Rossetti had a left breast mastectomy. The cancer had spread to three lymph nodes in her armpit, so it was necessary to remove the breast altogether. She chose not to look at what had been left of her flesh after the operation for nearly two weeks. When she did, she felt queasy and ill and had to sit on the lid of the toilet for quite some time in order to get herself together. The mastectomy had left her disfigured, like a soldier who'd been eviscerated by shrapnel or a Bouncing Betty.

The flesh would eventually heal in uneven, sometimes bifurcated patterns, and years later, from time to time, Rossetti would rest on the side of the tub and observe her wound with great and gentle motherly care. The left side of her torso, she thought, resembled a gargantuan extraction site of copper or silver, seen from high above the Earth. This made her happy and sad. In fact, she couldn't explain how or what she felt. The closest word she could find for what she felt was "melancholia."

Rossetti liked:

· tulips
· twice-cooked pork with hoisin sauce
· dress shoes
· purses
· cheap sunglasses, particularly those found on streets or beaches
· Jaguar cars
· stuffed grape or cabbage leaves
· Johnnie Walker (Red) whisky
· royal lineage (especially the Romanov family)
· Kent cigarettes
· Persian rugs
· flossing her teeth

- straight lampshades
- the sea
- Murano vases
- putting on airs of nobility
- telling little white lies that she called "ruby drops"
- Pavarotti singing "Nessun Dorma" from the final act of Puccini's opera, *Turandot*

Juan Weider's mother never again married. She reconnected with her high school sweetheart, a famous geologist who travelled around the world frequently to attend and give speeches at symposia, (most often he was the symposiarch himself) and was hardly ever in the country. But on the very rare occasions he was, they conducted a unique relationship—that of husband and wife in going about domestic tasks only. He would come home for lunch and she would fix a plate and sit with him. Neither would say anything. Then he would thank her, kiss her on the cheek, and go back to work.

While he was in Lausanne, Switzerland, giving a presentation on megathrust quake faults and the degree of weakness observed (stresses in subduction zones were found to be low, although the smaller amount of stress could still lead to a great earthquake), Rossetti felt severely short of breath and began to cough incessantly. She developed aggressive lung cancer and often had to go to hospital for thoracentesis (every three days). Each session, the nurse would remove between one and one-and-a-half liters of lung fluid. Sometimes the needle would have to be inserted into the pleural space to remove air, instead. It was all quite fascinating, although Rossetti did not think it so.

In the end, Juan Weider's mother could never explain to the geologist how she felt. The closest word she could find was "melancholia." But she never mentioned it. Instead she stressed the importance of the small details found in a day that constructed a tolerable life and routine. And so the geologist continued to travel for his work, outlining important events that were always breaking through the surface of his discipline: outlining the fingerprints of sea level rise, presenting the first global antineutrino emission map, the development of a new model of Amazon seasonal cycles, Earth's first CT scan, and so forth.

The geologist held onto Rossetti's ashes for nearly a year. The box, which was inside another cardboard, inconspicuous box looking very much like a small package of paperback novels, was placed on the bottom shelf of his bookcase. Throughout the time that it remained there, the geologist had every intention to honor Rossetti's last wishes: to be scattered onto the Black Sea and have a bouquet of sunflowers thrown in among the ashes. But he never brought himself to make the drive to the seaside.

One cold, winter morning, the geologist placed the box into his rubbish bin. He took the bag out into the hallway of his building, opened the chute, and dropped it down ten floors. The bag was incinerated later, along with all the other day's rubbish of the apartment building.

In spring of 2015, Juan Weider resurfaced briefly but only by a strange proxy, as if one were digging for truffles and came upon a nest of red ants. His body and flesh were not altogether there, but evidence of his fingerprints and footprints was discovered. Or to be more accurate, literally his fingers.

Earlier that year, a local Ecuadorian author named Fernando Nuñez del Arco alleged that the country had been the hiding place of ten important Nazi war criminals and several hundred more of lower rank. Of course, Juan Weider was nowhere on the author's list claiming this, as Juan Weider couldn't have been a Nazi during the war; he had been born twenty years after its end. Juan Weider, in fact if anything, would have loathed the fascists. In any case, Nuñez del Arco's insistence bordered on the maniacal, and so two investigators from the German government's official Nazi-hunting agency, the Central Office of the Investigations of National Socialist Crimes, came to investigate.

The two men came from Berlin with the Ecuadorian government's blessing. The investigators arrived in Quito and immediately went to work. They were: prosecutor Kurt Schrimm and police detective Uwe Blab. The men together physically, when standing side by side, invoked much laughter. Uwe Blab was nearly a giant, measuring six feet and ten inches.

Kurt Schrimm was his exact opposite. It wasn't known to anyone but Kurt Schrimm's wife, but he wore inserts inside of his shoes, which gave him two or so additional inches to his stunted heights.

The investigators were diligent, nevertheless, no matter how funny they looked together. For the first few weeks the pair focused on Ecuadorian public archives and registries in an attempt to track down surviving suspects (privately, the investigators did not believe any existed), but also to get at the historical truth of how Nazi war criminals found refuge in the South American country.

This part was significant because, although it had always long been known that many Nazis had fled to South America following the defeat of the Third Reich, attention had always focused on other countries like Paraguay, Argentina, Brazil, and Chile. Until Fernando Nuñez del Arco's allegations, Ecuador had largely flown under the radar.

Nuñez del Arco had always been a determined man. On the particular subject of unearthing his country's dirty secrets, he had been on a one-man mission. He spent five years researching his book *Ecuador and Nazi Germany*. This is what he claimed:

· Walter Rauff, inventor of the mobile gas chamber hid in Quito from 1948–1958.
· Gestapo chief Heinrich Muller also lived (but has probably died since) in Ecuador.

- Hitler secretly awarded Ecuador's foreign minister Julio Donoso the Order of the Eagle.
- Germany gave Quito a $34 million loan, seized from Jews.

Germany was a country that was always well respected culturally and very influential toward Ecuador, Nuñez del Arco said in his book. It held great prestige here while there was strong resentment in the US and UK, perhaps because of a kind of Hispanic-Catholic nationalism. The Nazis' influence in Ecuador was also strengthened by the fact that many senior officials in Quito at the time had studied in Germany before World War I. And during World War II, Germany was Ecuador's principal trading partner, with Hitler's war machine devouring raw commodities like balsa wood, rubber, coffee, and chocolate.

Nuñez del Arco had always been a thorough and determined man. One could even call him a savage detective. He went after his targets like a starving lion.

Upon their investigation of documents and government archives, the two German officials (Schrimm and Blab) came to the belief that the last Nazi to have been alive in Ecuador was of Dutch birth and that he died in Quito in 2008. But Nuñez del Arco had always been a determined man. He insisted they at least visit one small site in the Cayambe Coca Ecological Reserve forest at El Chaco. There, Nuñez del Arco claimed, they will see evidence of recent activity, perhaps of several years' residence.

What kind of evidence, Blab asked.

The usual kind. Discarded cans, packaging of foodstuffs, even traces of a fire pit that had been used consistently for an extended period of time.

The Germans travelled with the author and two guides—men with brown skin and wide, honest, sunburnt faces wearing colorful *ruanas*, alluding to their Pasto ancestors—to the small town of El Chaco. They were surprised to find a small but comfortable hotel called Guarida del Coyote. The establishment served strong coffee all day long. It also offered a large variety of omelets and freshly cut fruit.

This is a very fine little hotel, Schrimm said.

We have a very fine little country, you see, despite its dirty secrets, Nuñez del Arco smiled. Tomorrow we go see. And then you tell me whether the last Nazi died seven years ago.

The shack that Nuñez del Arco presented to the investigators (almost as if he were unveiling a new Mercedes Benz for an audience of buyers) had been abandoned for some time. Both Germans agreed with the author that someone had definitely lived there more recently than seven years previous. But the suspicion the investigators had was that the wooden shelter served in reality as the home base to a drug manufacturer—likely a *jefe* or a boss, not a notorious Fascist murderer on the run. They were sure they would find some type of homemade lab or evidence of coca processing not too far from the shack. They were convinced that the Ecuadorian had not looked thoroughly enough.

Here, you see, is the outhouse, Nuñez del Arco said. If you examine the dung inside the hole, it's soft still. The layer on top. It's soft. I pushed on it with a branch when I came across this dwelling earlier. And there, you see, is the fire pit I mentioned. The adobe is charred on the sides but from recent use. The soot is from recent fire. Do you agree.

Schrimm and Blab did.

I haven't looked close, Nuñez del Arco said, because I was excited to first come upon this treasure and, after all, the job of forensics cannot be done properly by a writer. A writer can research and can find. A writer can write. Sometimes he can even do it well. But you will look close. That is your profession. And you will find . . . I'm sure . . . I wonder what you will find. Gentlemen, Nuñez del Arco said proudly and inflated his chest, I wonder what you will find indeed.

Juan Weider had been there but had left days ahead of the expedition. The team of detectives had found his trail, but neither Schrimm nor Blab nor Nuñez del Arco or the guides had any idea who Juan Weider might have been. The evidence left behind, however, was more horrific than anything the Germans had seen in their inquiries throughout their entire careers. It wasn't the song of birds Juan Weider had been documenting so precisely in the shack discreetly tucked there in the Andean highlands. It wasn't that at all.

Right away Nuñez del Arco became giddy despite the images in the photographs and the rest of the physical evidence Schrimm and Blab excavated. He had, after all, found the work of a war criminal. You see gentlemen, what have I told you, he said.

Privately, the German investigators continued to believe that they had stumbled upon a narco's very modest hideout. The men were not at all as excited as their host who became more and more animated with excitement at the horror unfolding within the evidence. Nothing is beyond the capabilities of the monsters living inside us not quite too deep, Blab reasoned as he flipped through the photographs that documented the period Juan Weider had spent in the forest. There will never be a shortage of nightmares. The factory always stays open.

Now this one is interesting, Schrimm said. See here. He laid the small photograph on the wooden table and wiped off dirt from its glossy face. The print was maybe two inches by two inches, and its geometric edges were cut in an elegant pattern resembling sinusoidal waves connected together ad infinitum. Blab thought it very much resembled the symbol for infinity. It was meant to be a paper frame of sorts, like those used for historically famous paintings.

You see the fingers, Schrimm said. Blab squinted. The other German put a magnifying glass to the image. The hand captured on the emulsion was that of the photographer's, Juan Weider. It was placed in the scene on purpose in order to indicate the size and perspective of the terrifying objects on display for edification. They were all smaller than a fingernail.

Do you see the digits better now, Schrimm said again.

Yes.

Well, what do you notice.

Blab leaned in and adjusted the magnifying glass to better focus the image of the fingers. The hand is perfectly manicured, he said.

That's right, the other German said. And the fingers . . .

They're quite small and dainty, Blab said. Smooth, as well.

No rings.

Seems that way. No discoloration or tan lines or any sign of ever having had rings on them.

They are a woman's fingers nevertheless, Schrimm said. And a fairly young woman at that.

Blab agreed.

THOSE YEARS IN MONTREAL
(Published in Guernica, 2017)

WHEN DANIEL RECEIVED the phone call, he was lying in bed sweating out guilt and loneliness from the transgressions perpetrated in the humid Cleveland summer night. He lay next to a young woman who worked in the reception area at his engineering firm, and he picked up the receiver just before the second ring, praying to his on-again-off-again, conveniently summoned god that she would stay asleep. God answered: she did. He checked the dimly lit clock on the nightstand; its minute digit flipped slowly from seven to eight. The numbers were bathed in a pleasant amber light, and the slow change of digits made a quiet click. It was just past two in the morning.

The voice on the other end sounded very far away, a call maybe from his mother country where it would have been just after nine that same morning. It apologized for calling at such a late hour. Daniel didn't recognize the man, who excused himself again for the jarring call. But it wasn't a man. Milena Janowski briefly introduced herself as a clerk working alongside his ex-wife at the Ernest-Cormier building on Notre Dame Street in Montreal. And then she paused and began to sob softly. She excused herself, gathered her composure, mentioned her regret at the late hour again, and then she told Daniel that they had found Lily underneath all the mattresses. They were piled up high in the kitchen, three mattresses and two box springs, rising above a tremendous amount of rubbish, furniture, moldy food, cat litter soaked with urine and feces, spoiled milk, pizza boxes, magazines, newspapers, plastic utensils, months upon months—maybe a year—of hoarding and accumulating. When they got to Lily, it had been two days of constant debris removal by a professional firm. One of the men found her face down, crushed under the tower of mattresses wearing nothing. She must not have been dead for that long, Milena Janowski said, or maybe the horrendous stench already from the rotting things in the house simply masked the detritus of Lily's body. She did not know the details. They were in the medical report. She was so sorry, she said. In her will, Lily had left him a painting. There would have to be a period of time for probate, Milena Janowski said, close to a year, but the painting was an original by an artist called Ilfoveanu. Daniel would have to have it appraised, but she thought it was worth quite a sum. And would he mind paying tax on it as it crossed the border into the United States. Of course, he said. He would do whatever was required. Although they had not been married for quite some time, Daniel still thought fondly of Lily. There was a gap or a space in the telephone connection that widened quickly. Daniel heard the woman sob modestly again, this time from very far away. Once more he had the feeling she was calling from Poland. And then the line went dead.

He replaced the receiver and gathered himself up against the headboard. The young woman next to him sighed gently and turned her body and face away, toward the window. Her hair remained flat on one side. No one was in the room with him now. He thought of Lily. Those years in Montreal at the beginning were difficult and new, but enough time had passed since the complications of their marriage that Daniel felt the hole of melancholy begin to form in his stomach.

The first decent-paying job that Daniel had after he and Lily arrived was as a phlebotomy technician with AlphaMed on Avenue Dupuis, very close to Jewish General Hospital. In Krakow, Daniel had studied civil engineering at university and obtained a position within the layers of the Party designing public housing edifices, but now in their new world and their new lives there was more need for phlebotomists, according to the number of job openings in La Presse's classified section.

Lily did not like that Daniel worked so close to Jewish General Hospital. She did not like Jews.

While he trained for his certification, Daniel worked a fruit stand in Jean-Talon Market. The owner was a middle-aged Pole who lived with his mother in a two-room flat and was a member of an anti-communist group formed by the diaspora to support the newly established Solidarity at the Lenin Shipyards in Gdansk. The Pole paid in cash and political opinions at the end of each day, and in return for being a sympathetic audience Daniel was shown by his boss how not to pay taxes. Most of the money was spent on cartons of cigarettes he and Lily would consume instead of food. After a few weeks, they figured that it would be much cheaper to roll their own tobacco, so they bought a hand-rolling machine and used what they saved to buy scotch. A typical week's worth of food for both of them was a loaf of bread, 12 eggs, one quart of milk, and a stick of butter. At that time it cost them a little over $25 a month to eat. Lily said that the more they smoked the more they would suppress their appetites, thus saving money. It was something she'd been used to doing in their new world.

Daniel completed his training and became a certified phlebotomist in eighteen weeks. He began work at AlphaMed not only collecting blood, but also urine, semen, saliva, and sweat. During the certification courses, he was able to draw on his advanced training in Biology and Chemistry studied in his first year at university as part of his core studies, and the program seemed quite easy to complete. He did not think it would have to last so long. Some students, not so proficient in the sciences, opted to be trained in the longer version of the program: eight to ten months.

A few patients at AlphaMed were university students who needed extra pocket money, but most clients were transients, homeless, drug addicts, and prostitutes. Daniel didn't mind that so much, but Lily was constantly afraid that he would be robbed, beaten up, or even killed by the patients. This was a new world with new rules, she said. Daniel's shift was second—from three to eleven at night—and he walked to public transit after work. Lily waited for him every night. When he arrived safely, she would breathe with relief, pour two fingers of scotch for each of them, and smoke cigarettes. They wouldn't talk. Just sit at the kitchen table together and smoke. One evening he brought her a pineapple. She didn't know how to feel about that. Who brings home a pineapple after working with blood and cum and spit? And do they even have pineapples in Montreal? Later, she found the whole act of bringing her that gift very odd.

Several times during Daniel's stint as a phlebotomist at AlphaMed, he was accidentally stuck with needles that had just been used on patients. At that time no one knew anything about AIDS (it was still three years before the epidemic would be discovered and strike en masse), so Daniel didn't think the incidents were important enough to even mention to Lily. He'd just clean the puncture with alcohol and put a band-aid over it until the end of his shift. But a few years later when people started dying, he became concerned. He did not ever go for a test and he never told Lily about the instances. She was already quite anxious about most everything and often cried when she recounted her workday during their downtime in the afternoons over coffee. By that time he was out of phlebotomy and working toward obtaining an engineering degree from Ecole Polytechnique Montreal, as his formal education was not recognized by their new mother country. He surmised that if he hadn't had any symptoms by now, then nothing was wrong. He considered himself lucky, given who his patients were. Still, for years after, he would check himself thoroughly in the bathroom for lesions inside his mouth. Especially inside his mouth. He was obsessed with lesions appearing down in his throat. Those would be extremely tough to find. He used a flashlight to inspect the pink, meaty pockets that made up his gullet. In a way, the fleshy esophagus made him sick. He could never understand how doctors or surgeons could stand the look and feel of flabby meat. Nevertheless, he checked every day for lesions for many years.

Lily did her bit as well. She worked at BMO Bank of Montreal for a little over eight Canadian dollars an hour, which for those days wasn't too bad of a salary. She even had her own small office with a door just across the marble lobby and the tall bank of spaces where the tellers would stand and transact business. The manager was Luc Delahaye, an insignificant-looking older man who once may have been handsome but petite. He wore nice suits and smelled fresh, like soap. Luc Delahaye told Lily that if she needed quiet to concentrate on her numbers, she should feel free to close the door to her office. The lobby would sometimes get a bit too loud, especially at lunchtime or just after four in the afternoon on Fridays, and you never knew when all the hubbub would turn a 4 into a 9 or a 3 into an 8 on the balance sheet. That's what Luc Delahaye said in his quest to be kind.

Lily never closed her door. She liked looking out over the shiny marble at all the people waiting to move money. Money was an interesting animal to her. It was a tangible intangible. That's what she'd tell Daniel at the kitchen table sometimes. A tangible intangible with value assigned to it. It was all made up and it was all so interesting and depressing. Money. Just like time.

Once, when Luc Delahaye walked into her office to invite her to a lunch with a group of others, she saw his face glitch. It was the same kind of hiccup she'd been experiencing since her very first job in Montreal at PerfecLum. Only this glitch felt more severe, yet shorter than the others. A glitch is the only way she could describe it. As if she was watching television back in Poland and someone up on the roof violently bent or ripped out the antenna. But then quickly fixed it. The image broke then repaired itself. That's what Luc Delahaye's face did. It fractured, contorted, then put itself back together again. And there he was once more, smiling kindly and waiting for her answer to the lunch invitation. There was an audio glitch that went along with the picture break, as well. Snow or white noise filled her ears while the image broke. And then it all went away. It only took half a second. She told Daniel about it, but much later. By then the glitches were appearing more frequently, but she only told Daniel about this particular one with Luc Delahaye's face. They both thought it was amusing, and Daniel said it is probably the world having some technical difficulties again. And that the world would always right itself somehow.

Some time back, while Daniel was still working as a phlebotomist and coming home late, he sat down across from her at the kitchen table over cigarettes and said that maybe this world is one simulated computer program and all of us are just simply characters. Like in a play. Made up by someone. Said that life in their new home country was sometimes so ridiculous or absurd that it could likely be a software program with a large number of faults occurring. He was only joking, but Lily took that inside with her and never let it go.

They had an inside joke, the kind of short amusing one-two that, if told to anyone else, would elicit maybe a polite awkward snicker and the realization that neither of them were meant to have careers as funny people.

Which came first, the chicken or the egg?
The Lily.

Lily came first. She came late, maybe too late given that she'd had three opportunities in the years previous. In 1970 the Party released her passport and she traveled to Tripoli, in '73 the Central Committee again handed her the travel documents, and she flew to Mexico City. And in '76 she traveled to Detroit. The United States was the pearl, and she'd arrived in the country during celebrations for the bicentennial of its birth. Ironically, the opportunity to defect was greater in Detroit than the other foreign cities. Her handler was a sloppy man fond of Johnnie Walker Black, and every afternoon instead of supper he would stay in his room and start pouring fingers of the stuff, so that by early evening he was either out cold or incapacitated to such a degree that Lily and anyone else in the Polish economic delegation that had traveled to this marvelous motor city in decline could have simply walked out of the hotel and into the nearest FBI office.

She chose not to stay in any of those cities out of fear. Fear of the unfamiliar, of freedom, not the Party. By then the Party had become bored with itself. The world it had created came with too much paperwork. Bureaucrats were entrenched in so many administrative levels and were so bored out of their minds, that the Party had lost all its verve to survive. It loathed itself. If it took any action at all to combat a defection overseas, it would be some minor slap on the face of the defector's blood relations—usually an open, public meeting at which family members were shamed as cheats or weasels or rats.

Which came first, the chicken or the egg?

It was somewhat amusing, both she and Daniel thought, that it took four tries for Lily to come first. In the strange game of baseball, the rules say three chances squandered and you're out. In Lily's game, it was three strikes that allowed for yet a fourth chance. And on that one, she was in. She reached the base. Daniel had had no occasion to travel to the West and took every opportunity to mention to his wife that, had he been allowed by the Party to go, he'd have defected without trepidation that first time. He brought this up especially during their arguments, later, when they lived in their small flat on Ruelle Ontario. Daniel was resentful of the privilege allowed to his wife by the Party. And he was resentful of the chances she squandered before finally defecting that winter of '78. He thought they could have had a much better head start at a new life eight years before, when Lily received her first visa and her passport was released. An earlier head start and much younger.

She arrived in Montreal in late fall, 1978 as part of yet another economic delegation sent by the tractor and heavy machinery company at which she worked. All the delegation members joked at the idea of coming from a communist country in which the economy was planned in five-year blocks, to study a market-oriented economy that very much resembled that of the United States.

But Canada is socialist, just like back home, Eljbieta, the eldest in the group, said. And they all laughed on the flight over and ordered another round of drinks. After they got a little tipsy, they sang patriotic songs of their beloved Rzeczpospolita Polska in order to impress or placate their antsy handlers, while quietly making jokes about Comrade Leader Gomulka's supposed foreshortened physical endowment in the business of bed. It was the stuff that would once get you locked in prison or a work camp but, like the Party, the handlers were tired of it all. They were old gatekeepers in a system that had come to its natural conclusion.

All her life Lily had heard fantastic defection stories. There never seemed to be a dull one. The success stories always came out later, of course, after the brave ones made it to the other side, and as the tales traveled from one storyteller to another, they seemed to gather more and more extravagant details. There was the one in which an entire family sewed together bed sheets by hand for months, constructing a hot-air balloon. Instead of a basket, they attached three bucket seats from an uncle's Lada. The men all drew straws to decide which lucky (or unlucky) three would get to go, and the night they attempted the flight, the homemade ship lost a tremendous amount of altitude—so much, in fact, that as it quietly sailed past the snoozing border guard's shelter, one of the seats gently scraped the roof. The guard never flinched and the balloon made it over the border into West Berlin safely.

Then there was the one about the engineer in Gdansk who took to having ice cold baths every night for a year. He never uttered a word of explanation to his wife who eventually left him for an officer in the Polish army, thinking he had gone insane. But one night in the spring he pedaled to Nowy Port, chained his Wicher bike to a fence, and waded into the Gulf of Danzig in the Baltic. His outrageous plan was to swim in the cold waters all the way to Ystad, Sweden but miraculously, just off the shore of Leba as the engineer began to drown from exhaustion and hypothermia, a Danish ferry on its way to Riga spotted him and hauled him up on board.

Lily's defection story was nothing like the others she'd heard. It was simple and boring and, after some time giving it ample thought, she concluded that the door had been likely opened by the Party itself. No, her story was bland and short. Much like the simple truth of any real story. On the third night of the weeklong visit to Montreal, after supper at the hotel's restaurant, she placed her utensils on the side of her plate, removed the cloth napkin from her thigh, and left the dining room for the elevators. At the lobby, she turned left and walked out through the hotel revolving door with no other items or possessions other than what she wore. Simply walked out into the Montreal evening. She approached a Royal

Canadian Mounted Policeman, stated that she was a Polish citizen who faced persecution for her political beliefs, and asked for asylum.

Back home, Daniel made a huge fuss over the news. She had placed a call directly to their number in their flat, and listening to him scream and curse and lament about what she had done to their lives with this act of treason left her confused as to whether he was putting on a show for the case officers listening in or he was truly upset. It would have to be left alone for some other time when they could talk without surveillance by the Party.

During the ten months that she waited for Daniel to fight his end of the fight back in Poland and obtain a passport to be reunited under the Family Reunification Policy extended to political asylum refugees, Lily found a job at PerfecLum. It was a small family business run by a diminutive man named Thierry. PerfecLum manufactured lighting fixtures, and Lily worked above the warehouse in the purchasing department. In her position as a buyer, she would make decisions on which parts PerfecLum would procure from subcontractors in order to manufacture their lighting fixtures. Many of the employees in the warehouse depended on the purchasing department not just to keep buying parts, but to keep the prices on those parts very low. Their jobs were very precarious—often Thierry laid off workers because the purchasing department had gone over budget for the month and wouldn't be procuring parts until the following accounting cycle—and they all came to blame and despise Lily for their layoffs.

Lily hated being put in that kind of position, and she would come home to her efficiency flat, sit at the small table, smoke cigarettes and cry. Her dinners were one boiled egg and a can of sardines. The man downstairs made horrific noises in the middle of the night. Sounded like he was being eviscerated by an axe. It would go on for hours. The glitches Lily began experiencing quite often reassembled into the image of her neighbor, nude and on all fours, growling at her with a bloody mouth. His genitals were exposed and wounded, as if he had been neutered like a pet dog. She despised this life and thought about going back. What could they do that was worse than this new immigrant life.

Daniel was allowed to receive phone calls from her and would make all sorts of demands regarding his own case. He would talk for hours about paperwork and bureaucracy and how much he was made to suffer because of Lily's defection. The line was under surveillance all the time, and Lily could never truly figure out whether all of it was a show for those listening in. The international calls cost Lily a fortune. She began to skip eating in order to be able to pay the bill. But she never told Daniel. Not even later, during their fights. He went on and on lecturing, complaining, moaning about his frustrations, his nightmares. He was under surveillance all the time now. They were not even attempting to be discreet. He had been demoted and now was threatened with outright expulsion from the engineering department. He was humiliated. He had a stain on his name. That's what he said. He had a stain on his character and everyone knew it. He had lost all of their friends. And Lily listened and tried soothing him anyway she could and skipped eating. One month, during the brutal winter, she went without a meal for six days straight. Just water and cigarettes.

Despite all, she was able to buy a small, used car. Only two hundred dollars. She took a Polaroid in front of it and sent it to Daniel. She was proud of her little Chevette. Later, an angry letter arrived from him, fuming about the egregious spending on such a luxury and accusing Lily of having a grand old time buying cars while he was being psychologically tortured, his life ruined. Once again she couldn't tell whether this was posturing for the censors. She never truly had a firm idea of what Daniel was thinking during those ten months they were apart. Her glitches continued.

Then, one sunny late autumn day Daniel called to tell her that he'd been cleared to leave. Just like that, out of nowhere. There was no explanation or details. He was calling from the Telephony Ministry, from one of their international calling booths. The line clicked and the conversation on his end was often interrupted by blank, quick spaces. He told her the call was extremely expensive and he had only been able to afford buying two minutes. He would write with departure details next day. It came from nowhere just like that. The news stunned her. After she hung up she couldn't feel happy about it. Something wasn't right. The persistent wall of bureaucracy that had been in place all those months ongoing suddenly crumbled. Daniel sounded strange in between the clicks and clacks of the tapped line. He sounded less afraid and weary; in fact he seemed cocky. She could only feel as if she had been sentenced to hang and at the very last moment, as she was being led up to the gallows, the execution had been cancelled. Maybe that wasn't such a great example after all.

In the first week of Daniel's arrival in Montreal, he decided they would get rid of the small economy car. In its place they bought a used 1978 Ford Fairmont. It was brown, had four doors, automatic transmission, rear-wheel drive, an eight-cylinder engine, and—although it was a spacious American car—it was assembled in Ontario. The best of both North American worlds. He was proud. Daniel felt the car had enough clout for a couple of Polish immigrants to legitimize their standing in the new country. Now they were like most others. The pain of starting over from nothing was ameliorated by the spacious automobile. In subsequent letters to friends and distant family in Warsaw and Krakow, as well as Lily's own relations in Poznan, Daniel would always include a photograph of the car: prosperity.

In the beginning, they took many recreational trips in the Ford Fairmont. Once, as far west as Cleveland, Ohio. A grade school friend of Daniel's who had failed to pass the baccalaureate out of high school and moved to Wroclaw to fix combines and tractors, had miraculously emigrated with his wife and small daughter to the United States, and the family was now living in Berea. The St. Stanislaus Church on Forman Avenue sponsored the family's immigration and donated most everything they owned in the small flat. Neither Daniel nor Lily truly liked this family. The lack of formal education placed their status much lower on the sliding social scale to which everyone from the mother country adhered, even here in the New World. It was ridiculous to apply the old standards to people sometimes literally standing in the same boat as you, sailing the same waters. But Daniel and Lily held to their views, all of them tethered to the Ford Fairmont.

They visited Niagara Falls. Everyone said the Horseshoe Falls on the Canadian side, their side, was by far the most majestic. All the Canadians liked that. It trumped their neighbor, and there was nothing to be done about it. Lily and Daniel felt proud. They drove a bit up along the Niagara River and found a rest area with a small bench just on the shore of the sprinting white waters. Daniel talked of the river, which drains Lake Erie into Lake Ontario, as if it were an old peasant with strong legs and back. Horseshoe Falls is the most powerful waterfall in North America as measured by vertical height and flow rate. The vertical drop is more than 165 feet. What is that in meters, Lily said. About fifty. The flow is incredible because of its width; it's not too impressive in height. But the width . . . more than six million cubic feet of water falls over the crest line every minute. What is that in meters, Lily said. 168,000 cubic meters. Daniel suggested she learn the conversion rate and pretended to scold her, wagging his finger. They kissed just then. It was all awkward.

There are tales, they are famous, of suicidal people going over the falls in barrels, Daniel said. I don't know if they're true. A few of those people even survived the drop. Lily laughed. She thought it was all legend, on par with the fantastic defection stories from the motherland. Probably is, Daniel said. They unfolded the wax paper carefully, making sure to not tear it so it could be reused, and ate their bologna sandwiches right next to the rushing waters of the river, on the bench.

Lily didn't like Toronto. They visited twice in the Ford Fairmont, and both times Lily might as well have held her nose the duration of the trips. Toronto was dirty and dangerous, especially around the CN Tower, which had just been erected a few years before. There was trash blowing on the streets around the tower. Lily found the city big, stark, cold, and uncivilized. On the other hand, Daniel thought Toronto was probably the closest to New York City he'd ever get. He loved everything about it. He loved its cold, brutal architecture; it reminded him of concrete communist apartment and government buildings back home in Krakow. He loved the litter blowing around like leaves on the drafty streets, especially down close to the water. It was a metaphor for freedom. People were free to pick them up or let them blow around. Better yet, people were free to discard them in the first place. It was people's prerogative what to do about it. Everything about Toronto said "muscle." Everything about it said, "Boy, you've arrived in the West."

They went up to the observation deck of the CN Tower, leaned against the steel bars of the protective cage, and looked down upon the city. Daniel had taken Lily to the cinema to see a romantic comedy film called Highpoint. There's a scene in which a man falls off the tower from exactly the deck on which they were now peering down. Dar Robinson is the name, Daniel said. What. Dar Robinson is the guy's name. What guy. The real guy who did the jump from here, Daniel said. In the movie. Dar Robinson. He's the stuntman. Oh, Lily said. It's crazy, isn't it. What people do sometimes. It is. Lily thought again about the defection stories she'd heard. She couldn't imagine anyone jumping off the tower for no reason. Money, that's the reason, Daniel said. And that was the trip up the CN Tower in Toronto, that summer of 1982.

That was the summer of betrayal. That's what Lily called it privately, to herself on nights alone at the table, sitting with her cigarettes and her scotch.

In August they had a visitor. The eldest daughter of the family living in Cleveland came to stay with Daniel and Lily for six weeks before the start of her first year of high school. Their flat was small, but it did have two bedrooms, so they installed the girl in the guest room and made sure she had as much of the comforts for a long-term visiting guest as they could provide.

Her Polish name was Despina. She was named after Despoina, a nymph who was a daughter of Poseidon and Demeter. But in America she went by Lavinia. It was such a strange choice, this switch from Greek to Roman mythology. In Roman folklore, Lavinia was the daughter of Latinus and Amata and the last wife of Aeneas. Lavinia, the only child of the king and "ripe for marriage," had been courted by many men who hoped to become the king of Latium. There is a not-so-world-famous yet astounding painting from 1565 by Mirabello Cavalori depicting the memorable moment in Book VII of the *Aeneid* during the scene of sacrifice at the altar of the gods when Lavinia's hair catches fire—an omen promising glorious days to come for Lavinia and war for all Latins. But also an omen for ultimate reconciliation. Cavalori's painting is called *Lavinia at the Altar*. It resides in the Palazzo Vecchio in Florence.

Her days ran long. Each morning, pretending she was still asleep in her room, Lavinia would wait for Daniel and Lily to go through their morning motions then finally, quietly leave for their jobs, before she would emerge into the empty flat, make breakfast, and turn on the small television set in the kitchen.

Lavinia's sleeping habits were nothing like what one would expect of a teen. She often suffered from insomnia, which was further buttressed in its brutal toll on the mind and body by a tendency to awaken very early the following morning, thus only allowing her two or three hours of sleep. Lavinia learned to tolerate quiet and loneliness by waiting for dawn in bed and singing to herself various popular songs played on the radio. That summer, the summer of betrayal, she ached immensely, for no radio station in Montreal carried Casey Kasem's America's Top Forty program, and for nearly a month she had absolutely no idea what new songs had entered into the countdown or fallen out of it, nor what shuffling happened in the top ten. She felt disconnected. Those days in Montreal ran long. And so she wrote letters back home.

Dear Mama and Tata,

I hope you are both well and keeping your health. I am having a good summer, thanks to you (thank you for the money), although it's surprisingly hot up here. Out of curiosity, I looked on the map and found that our mother Poland is only slightly higher in latitude than Montreal. It doesn't make much sense for it to be so stifling here, although the flat has two ceiling fans, one in each bedroom and so it makes living through the afternoons bearable. Daniel and Lily have been very nice to me. Each morning they tiptoe around the flat in order not to wake me and whisper their conversations. They try very hard. (And, really, it's not necessary as I am awake anyway, you know how I sleep. Or don't. Haha.) Even if I were to be still asleep, their consideration is useless for the very first thing they do when they come out of their room is cough incessantly. It is probably the countless cigarettes they smoke. They use a small machine to roll their own cigarettes. It's quite interesting. I don't know why they do that when they can buy packs in cartons already rolled perfectly. In any case, it's a horrendous racket. One of them sounds like a donkey who has been shot and is slowly dying. This coughing goes on for nearly a quarter of an hour from the both of them. It's amusing. At times it's like they're both competing against one another in a strange sort of cough-off. At others it almost seems they are striving to coordinate their hacking as if in a choir. And then it just suddenly stops and the whispering begins. Those are my mornings. After they've gone, there isn't too much to be done. There is television with the same channels and programs that we have, so I fix myself some toast and tea and watch until close to noon. There are some other shows in French, and sometimes I'll watch them just to hear another language. But it's not the French that we know. It's a strange type of French. I don't know how to properly describe it. It's "dirtier." Something is not quite right with it. You would have to hear it for yourselves. In any case, I have found an old tennis ball so the last few days after I eat my soup for lunch I have made it a habit to go downstairs in the courtyard and throw the ball against the wall of the apartment building. After that, I usually walk around the area just to kill some time. There are some boys with skateboards who jump stairs and do some other tricks, and sometimes I'll sit and watch them. They are Montreal boys. They speak that same kind of "dirty" French I just told you about. Other than that, it is pretty much how I fill my days here. Daniel and Lily have promised to take me to Niagara Falls soon. And to a used book store, because I have finished reading all three novels you've packed with me.

With love from Montreal,
With love and kisses,
Your daughter,
Despina

During that summer of betrayal, the glitches visited Lily more frequently. And they began to show up also during her sleep at nights. They weren't dreams; they were distinct in their horror. Lily could tell the difference. They were glitches appearing while she dreamt, independent or alongside of her reverie. There was a difference, and she could tell within a dream when a glitch was occurring. It seeped into the dream and took over like the roots of a weed, finally waking Lily, jarring her forward, heart pounding so loudly it sounded as if a marching band bass drum was being struck next to her ears. She often took Valium and scotch to ameliorate the horror and weirdness. There was nothing more she could do. And there was nothing more she would say to Daniel about his betrayal.

For his part, he went on as if nothing had happened. Was happening. He rolled their cigarettes each morning, he even made the tea and toast, he bathed, he shaved, he dressed, he went to work. It wasn't ideal, but it was better than other immigrant lives he'd heard of. Theirs was a life most ordinary, given they had started with nothing and from nothing, and that's all they could ask for. An ordinary life in Montreal was something to write proudly home to.

Dear Mama and Tata,

I hope this letter finds you happy and healthy. Thank you for wiring the money. Lily was kind enough to drive me to a used book store and I found a copy of Tom Sawyer for 15 cents! It's yellow and smells musty but I don't care. It was 15 cents! Something strange is happening between the three of us now. It began with a peculiar incident involving Daniel just last week, but in the few days since, things have changed. It happened during a regular morning. Everything was the same as any other morning: the coughing, the courteous whispers given the early hours, quiet feet sliding around the flat, the smells of toast, jam, etc. Then the door closed and the familiar quiet imbibed the flat. I decided to stay in bed a little longer. There was, as usual, not much to do and I was tired of chucking a ball at a wall all day. I suppose I began to daydream. I don't know how much time went by, but suddenly I heard keys turning in the lock and the door to the flat was opened quietly. The feet were heavier moving around, though they tried to keep hushed, and I knew it was Daniel. Maybe he'd forgotten something. There's nothing suspicious about something like that, is there. I just lay there listening. There was the familiar sound of cupboards and drawers being opened, all with great care not to make too much noise. I assume that he assumed I was still asleep. I heard the refrigerator door open and close several times. It was all so strange. What could he have forgotten that he checked for it in the refrigerator so many times. The interval between the footsteps got shorter and shorter, so I only assumed the search for whatever it was he needed intensified. Again and again: more drawers sliding open, more cupboards. Then the utility closet door squeaked, so he was looking in there, as well. All of this went on for God knows how long. I didn't want to move and look at my watch, which was on the desk a few feet away. The telephone made a little "ding" when the receiver was lifted off the hook, and then I heard the dial being rotated. Whoever it was that Daniel spoke to must have been in a hurry because the conversation was very short. I couldn't hear any of it because things were strictly whispered, not that I probably could have understood anyway. I have never been good at guessing things like that and it was, after all, a one-way discussion I was hearing. Or not hearing, haha. Then, again, the weirdness. He placed the receiver on the hook (the telephone made that little "ding" again) and there was quite a long time that passed without any sound. I did not know what he could have been doing. Maybe standing there thinking. Suddenly I heard two little squeaks of the floorboards just outside my room, and I knew Daniel was standing on the other side of the door *quietly. I closed my eyes and held my breath. I don't know why I did that. A person pretending to be asleep can't possibly not breathe. But I did it. I heard nothing for a long time. Maybe it wasn't so long but it seemed like an eternity knowing Daniel was just outside my door listening. So I decided to make it sound even more real. I began to snore a little. The floorboards yelped again. I felt the door slowly being unlatched by the handle. I cracked open one eye just enough to discern shapes. The door had been opened a few inches and I saw Daniel standing there in the small width of vision offered by the door. He stood and watched me snore (eyelids still slightly apart) for at least five minutes. I did not know what was going to happen next. I had not known Daniel to be aggressive or improper in any way, during the time I've spent here. I expected he would step in for some reason. Maybe quietly open the nightstand drawer next to my head. But he didn't. He didn't do anything. Just stood and watched. I felt we were participating in a duel of fraud. Whose willpower was going to give out first? His, finally deciding to take some action. Or mine, pretending to wake up as if everything was normal, hopefully chasing him away from his peculiar mission. I would do it slowly, to give him a chance to close the door and vacate the flat. But I also was curious. I wasn't afraid. What did he want from me. I say this again: please know I never felt I was in any kind of danger. I persevered, feigning unconsciousness. Finally, gently, he pulled shut the door and made sure the latch caught without clicking. I heard him move toward the living room, open the front door, and pull it behind him very quietly. He turned the deadbolt gently. And that was the end of it. I held very little hope of maybe finding out what this was all about later in the evening when they'd be home and I could watch them together, giving some kind of clue in their interaction. And I was right. The rest of the day went on as usual. Next week I am coming home, as you know, but I'll keep you posted if anything extraordinary should happen. I have the permission to call you both any time I wish.*

With love and kisses,
Your daughter,
Despina

p.s. Tell Andrzej to stop biting his nails. He has already passed through 6th grade, there is nothing to worry about in 7th. Nothing is new.

INTERVIEWER: Then there was the . . . uh, the summer. Was it? Or was it—no. (papers rustling) Summer, yes summer.

LILY JELEN: I don't . . . the summer?

INTERVIEWER: Right. What was it . . . how did you put it?

LILY JELEN: I don't know if I follow you. What summer?

INTERVIEWER: You called it, uh . . . let me look through my notes. Uh. Just . . . give me a . . . You named it . . .

LILY JELEN: Oh, sure sure. Yes. The Summer of Betrayal. (scoffs)

INTERVIEWER: That's right. The summer of betrayal.

LILY JELEN: In capital letters. (now laughs)

INTERVIEWER: (hums ominously, they both laugh) Tell me about the Summer of Betrayal, capital S, capital B.

LILY JELEN: Well . . . it's really quite simple. Really, if you think about it, think about where we're coming from. Well? There's nothing unique. I might be more upset now with myself that I gave it such importance. If I think about it . . .

INTERVIEWER: Tell me.

LILY JELEN: Yes. Well, yes. Like I said. That was the summer I found out Daniel was an informer.

INTERVIEWER: An informer. What's an informer, can you tell me. Just . . . for this (clicking noises heard).

LILY JELEN: Yes . . . a man, well doesn't have to be a man, can be anyone. Children even. Daniel informed for the Esbecja. That was the Polish secret police. It was called the Security Service of the Ministry of Internal Affairs. But we called it Esbecja.

INTERVIEWER: And . . . (unintelligible noise) so Daniel was a spy?

LILY JELEN: (laughs gently) Well. I suppose in a very tangential, official way. But (more laughing quietly) . . . in reality a very minor way. What I mean, he wasn't important enough or trained enough to be a spy. He was just an informer. He would watch and listen to what I said or how I was around him and then he would make reports that somehow would end up with the Esbecja. And probably it wasn't just me he was informing on. His own colleagues, as well.

INTERVIEWER: He would write reports on you and others?

LILY JELEN: I don't know quite for sure about the others. Probably . . . The things he informed on, on me, I mean, those things were just the boring things. You know. Went to work, bought this product, came home, ate this, drank that, smoked these kinds of cigarettes. Those sorts of things. The kinds of things one doesn't remember on a daily basis. So I think, yes. He was making out reports of some kind. There must have been paper.

INTERVIEWER: These are the details the Polish secret police is interested in? In their émigrés?

LILY JELEN: (laughs) You would not believe what the secret police is interested in.

INTERVIEWER: Tell me.

LILY JELEN: Anything. Everything. Perverted, especially. Fetishes, preferences, noises made in bed. They want to know where you go, who you meet with, what you talk about, how you brush your teeth, what kind of toothpaste you use . . . they even . . . they want to know when you have your period and what kind of tampons you use.

INTERVIEWER: So . . . (unintelligible sounds/garbled)

LILY JELEN: . . . because once I feigned sleep and saw him look through the bathroom rubbish. He pulled out the applicator, turned it, flipped it . . . and it seemed he was looking for a brand name.

INTERVIEWER: That's . . . is that normal?

LILY JELEN: Well, yes. I don't know. Yes. I'm sure. There are worse things than snooping through rubbish for private matters, though. Many have done those things in order to get information on someone.

INTERVIEWER: But . . . and help me understand.

LILY JELEN: Why?

INTERVIEWER: (laughs) Yes! Why? Why this irrelevant minutia?

LILY JELEN: I don't know. They just want to know everything about everyone. Especially émigrés abroad.

Probably to have something to compromise you with. Later. Or your family back home. You know, when they need you for something. To use you for something. They show you pictures—doctored pictures—or they drop a hint in the conversation, or they leave a note. To compromise your integrity or . . . strong arm you into doing whatever they want. Or just to intimidate you. It's terrifying to have a total stranger come up and tell you he knows when your time of the month comes and the type of tampons you use. It's really . . . it's menacing. It subdues you. The fear. It just grapples with you. And you know that you're not alone. Or free. That's how they can control you even overseas. And hope to turn you. Into an informer, I mean.

INTERVIEWER: So . . . then, other people . . .

LILY JELEN: Oh, many other people are informers. Here. In the United States. Everywhere. In every country there are people informing for others in other countries.

INTERVIEWER: No, I meant why would Daniel inform on other people? You mentioned he probably did. His colleagues, for example?

LILY JELEN: Yes. Well. I don't know why others would be interesting to the Esbecja.

INTERVIEWER: Same kind of information?

LILY JELEN: Whatever they want, I suppose.

INTERVIEWER: What about . . . (papers shuffling) how about that incident with the lunchtime guest? Tell me about that.

LILY JELEN: Yes. Well. That was . . . I mean a lot of these case officers are . . .

INTERVIEWER: Case officers?

LILY JELEN: Yes. Each informer is assigned a case officer. Someone from back home. Someone who works for the Esbecja. Informers themselves are promoted to case officers, depending on the type of job they do. Or information they get. These people, usually, these case officers are not too bright, you know. In general. Most of them are older men set in their ways. Broken down men. They work for other older men also set in their ways. And also broken. Who work for other older men, and so on. There are so many levels to the bureaucracy that a lowly case officer assigned to an informer such as Daniel—you know, an informer with not very interesting information on a regular woman—they just . . . these people aren't very bright. That's all.

INTERVIEWER: What happened?

LILY JELEN: It was really absurd. (laughs) So dumb. I had to rush home at lunchtime. Well, after, really. I think it was food poisoning. Anyway, I could never . . . I never was comfortable using the washroom at work for these types of things. And, at that time I could walk and be home in only a few minutes. Of course that meant . . . well, I was much more comfortable at home. So then . . . well, anyway, uh . . . I just walked in on him. Simply. God, he just . . . he just looked so thick standing there. He and that other fellow.

INTERVIEWER: Do you remember . . .

LILY JELEN: Mikolaj . . . uh, Mikolaj something. You know. Nicholas in English.

INTERVIEWER: And you knew this man.

LILY JELEN: Daniel knew him in Poland. So I knew him through Daniel. It wasn't too big a secret that he was an informer. Just . . . it was surprising. That he would get caught like that.

INTERVIEWER: You both knew that he worked for . . . that he informed in Poland?

LILY JELEN: Yes. We talked about it then. That's why this entire thing, uh . . . incident. It's so dumb. All of it. Here was this fellow who informed back home, now here suddenly. In our flat. In Montreal. A case officer for Daniel.

INTERVIEWER: And then?

LILY JELEN: Daniel had this dumb look on his face. This weird smile . . . it was . . . crooked and forced. Somehow. Crooked with . . . crookedness. But also deceitfulness and the stupidity of that. The stupidity of lies and being caught in them. I had just walked in on the two of them. So easy and simple. They had been talking right there in the kitchen. I could hear them as I was turning the key. Imbeciles. Both of them. Just . . . such imbeciles. Couldn't be discreet. Couldn't have met somewhere out, like they all usually do. They were caught by the person they were watching. Who came home to use the washroom. It's a good end to a career in espionage and propaganda (scoffs).

INTERVIEWER: What did Daniel say?

LILY JELEN: (laughs) Just, uh . . . he struggled with something about the Catholic Church having just sponsored the immigration of Mikolaj. He was loaning him money. That was the story. Daniel was loaning him money to get started. And God, the other imbecile. You know he actually took my hand and kissed it? With his dry, thin lips and that gaunt prison face. That . . . I don't know. Liars all look the same, don't they. The entire thing was so stupid and awkward. And then it was over. The fellow left.

INTERVIEWER: Did you see him again? Did he come back or . . . ?

LILY JELEN: No.

INTERVIEWER: At all?

LILY JELEN: Never again. I never spoke about it and neither did Daniel. It was just . . . it was just understood. I expected him to even maybe shrug. You know . . . as if: eh. That's the way things are. And . . . that is the way things were. It had traveled with us, this . . . well. All of it. It reached here, too. We brought it with us. That's what we were good for. Like I said, it's all over and in America, too.

INTERVIEWER: Is that when you left him?

LILY JELEN: Daniel would probably like to say we had left each other.

INTERVIEWER: Would he be right?

LILY JELEN: No. He'd left a long time before. He left in Poland.

INTERVIEWER: And you did not want to be betrayed obviously?

LILY JELEN: No, well . . . I don't know how to put this. It was more . . . the betrayal, yes. All right. But, really . . . just the stupidity of it. And how I fell for it. Or . . . for how long . . . I don't know how to say this fully. I felt . . . unintelligent. Naive. It's what really did it. Being so clueless and . . . at the hands of

Daniel. And for nothing. I mean, nothing of value. I had nothing of value for him to report on. I couldn't look at his face afterwards. This person who went through my trash every night. We stayed together for a while, but I wouldn't look at his face from that moment on.

INTERVIEWER: Do you think that's why they let him come? I mean you mentioned it was strange and sudden when he called you that day with the news that he'd been allowed to leave.

LILY JELEN: Yes. That's when they turned him. The betrayal, the . . . well, the vacuous thing about it is that he didn't have to do anything at all after he arrived here. After we were together here in Montreal.

INTERVIEWER: You don't think he would have been in some sort of danger if he reneged on the deal?

LILY JELEN: (laughs) Nobody would have cared. At that time, or . . . by that time nobody really cared anymore. I mean, back home. It was all coming to an end. Everyone knew it. Everyone in the system had had it. It was going to be over. Most people were bored. Or old. I didn't matter. Daniel didn't matter. If he backed out on his deal, whatever that was, no one would have done anything. That's the absurd part. He didn't have to do it. He didn't have to crush me like that. God, how pea-brained I felt. And for so long after. Still now, even . . .

INTERVIEWER: Were you separated or divorced during the cancer treatments?

LILY JELEN: I don't remember. Daniel may have been gone already to the States by then. I don't . . . I think maybe divorced. It didn't matter. I didn't need anyone to help me.

INTERVIEWER: And what kind of cancer?

LILY JELEN: Breast. (some rubbing noise on the mic) Left radical mastectomy. (more noise) And all the lymph nodes under the left arm. (coughing) I can't lift above . . . (more coughing/incessant/retching sounds) I can't . . .

After it was over for them, some time passed before Lily finally began to call Daniel. Though contentious in the early days, the split was fairly amicable, so the conversations on the phone were somewhat friendly and common, if not strange. The calls came mostly in the late evenings or at night. She sounded drugged or drunk most of the time. Daniel never asked; he just listened. For a long time after the split, he felt it was part of his atonement for what he had done to her. There were other components Daniel felt he should endure, but that meant he had to approach the idea of there being a higher power and answering to it strictly. Or bowing before it in an attempt to expiate. He chose to listen to Lily as often as she would call, in whatever altered state she happened to be, whatever the reason. That's how, he decided, he would pay back her debt.

Her ditties were excruciating: mundane details and stories that would never get anywhere. That Sunday in the pool when she jumped in and tried to merely cross it widthwise, and somewhere in the middle of the very short voyage she couldn't go on any longer. She ran out of breath and nearly drowned. If it wasn't for Larry the lifeguard, she'd have been gone. And did you know Larry the lifeguard is studying to become a surgeon? The IBM Selectric she used to summarize monthly reports was not registering the letter "I" correctly. Only the bottom half with its serif showed up on paper. And what could that mean. (She would have to complete the letter with a black ink pen later on the paper.) Gourds at the Jean-Talon Market all looked like mangled grenades. Was that a message for her from the farmers who grew these fleshy, weird fruits. The lawyer handling her citizenship case demanded an extra thousand dollars over what was agreed. She could, he proposed, work for it by typing court transcripts for him.

The calls continued into the years stretching out beyond the disbanding of their union. After Daniel settled in the US, he debated whether he should continue to listen to the now strange and very long expostulations. There was little doubt something was not right with Lily. The guilt had not abated for Daniel, though he was now beginning to rationalize the certain choices he had made in his life. That would be a first step to an eventual decision. But it wouldn't be inaccurate to say his wish would be that whatever it was eating Lily from the inside would consume her quicker.

One evening he had drunk too much white wine and was feeling numb and useless. The phone rang. Lily was agitated but not yet irate. She would become so over the next two hours of the mostly one-way conversation, Daniel knew that. On this night, though, he didn't feel like enduring her any longer. He had been listening to a record and having an all right time drinking by himself. When he picked up the receiver and heard Lily's voice, that shrill, piercing sound made by a larynx that he had learned to dislike so much lately, ignited an avalanche of anger, impatience, guilt at feeling the first two, and finally a just rationalization for what he was about to do: nothing too dramatic or extreme, but enough to maybe send a final message. He set down the phone next to the stereo speaker, microphone end closest, flipped the long-playing record to its second side, put down the needle into the first groove, and left.

Some time, much later, clock moving toward the early morning hours, Daniel returned to the location of the deed in order to return everything to their normal places. The record had long ago stopped spinning. He picked up the needle and replaced it in its cozy U-shaped holder, turned off the power at the stereo amplifier component, and picked up the telephone. He brought it up to his ear on instinct only (it was a precaution he had been taught while young; phone manners in the mother country were vital and one never wanted to close the connection without properly ensuring that the party on the other end was ready to oblige), and realized the line was still open. Was Lily listening? Or had she passed out from whatever substance was flowing through her, without hanging up. He listened to his end for several minutes. There was nothing but the open line. Finally, he returned the receiver to its cradle. He did so gently, fearful that he would stir awake the monster on the other end, which might have dozed off with the receiver at her ear. That was the last he heard from Lily. The calls just simply ceased. And then he completely lost track of her.

He was running on the burdened and exhausted legs of the very early morning. The clock on the nightstand laboriously flipped over its digit and he was now into the four o'clock hour. It was useless to try to sleep. Too late. Make it up tomorrow, maybe. The woman next to him sighed and stirred softly. Daniel was envious. She was ensnared into that blissful dream-state that had eluded him most of his adult life. The real substance of a dream, however, is the submersion into dread. It's why the dreamer doesn't quite remember much in the morning; the psychic defense mechanism kicks in like a generator, erasing all traces of horror. Still, Daniel was jealous of her trance. He would have to soon awaken her so that she had ample time to gather herself together enough that she wouldn't arouse suspicions at the office. They would, of course, meet up again like this and go on pretending no one knew about their affair.

Insomnia, Daniel knew, is the existential equivalent of infinity. He also knew that for the first time in years he no longer had the remotest idea of what he knew. It was coming to the end of the decade, soon it would be the end of the great century, and the fashion was rising in society to inquire after what had transpired, and what the new millennium was to bring next. Daniel had been a poor prophet of that time—the time from when he was born to now. But it was not a century for prophets, poor a prognosticator as he had been. It didn't matter that he never had foresight or hindsight. The last one hundred years had not been for him or Lily. The century had been for the ones who used people like him or Lily. The rest was breadcrumbs thrown on the floor to be fought over: the used took advantage of one another, sometimes knowingly, agreed upon in the form of an elementally understood contract. The used used the used. If anyone was left with anything, it was a burden of regrets and failures. For those people, most people, the century had yielded nothing.

Earlier, on the phone, Milena Janowski had said Lily bequeathed him a work of art. It seemed all very peculiar for a gift of the estate to be sent to him after so much time of no contact. Though it had only been a couple of hours, Daniel felt the conversation took place days ago, weeks even. A painting,

Milena Janowski had said, bequeathed to him. A painting that had to be registered and paid for at customs.

He shifted and stood on the side of the bed, quietly, feet on the cool floor. The early morning air of the room was heavy and thick with humid dreams and recollections. Blood flowed from his head into his thighs and all systems began to kick on. Daniel wondered what kind of taste in art Lily had developed over the last years. She was always a sophisticated woman. But that, too, disappears with time. A painting . . . of what or whom. Would it mean anything to him, really. And then he knew. He would never receive the artwork. And he would never set to inquire after it, either.

INFEST
(Published in The Talking Book, 2016)

THEY'RE IN THE WALLS. Bugs or rats or. Bats. At night they come most alive and torment with bites or bits or pitter-patter of feet or claws or. Iron. Crawling within the spaces next to the beds. They plant ideas for which men and women are arrested. Crimes to which people confess. It all comes from inside the walls. Insomnia and fear. Rats and bugs and mice and. Inequities. Boots. People in this part of the world sleep with boots on. In the event Mother comes, she comes at night and if anything, one must have boots for Mother. Even if hauled away naked. But no. People sleep fully clothed with identification papers in breast pockets, suitcases packed. And good, strong boots. Those are the nights. They wait for Mother. Sometimes it takes years. But she comes in the end.

Mother. In the meantime, there is hot water on Wednesdays and Fridays.

(ready camera two . . . take camera two)

The young woman caretaker says: come on, sweets. Come. Bundle up. Right here, up here. Wrap this round like this. On your neck. Come on, now. And the hat. And mittens too. Come on, you chicken. The toddler spins around and unravels herself from the scarf still held by the woman and giggles. Then she spins the opposite way and wraps it back up again halfway on her face. And the hat now, says the woman. Hat splat, the child says and blows a raspberry. Giggles. Another raspberry. More giggles. Now the woman: she's being a little pest again. Who's the pest. Little pest walking in the walls, little pest ripping up her dolls. Come, let's go. The girl giggles and spins around and around. She stops, claps, and something in the corridor rings. It's feedback. From the bugs. In the flat.

(ready camera one . . . take camera one, open all mics)

From inside the fogged windows of the trolleybus, the marquis signs on the buildings along Boulevard Scala look like fleeting rabbits or out-of-focus prairie dogs in pursuit of a semicolon that feeds. The young woman caretaker leans in close to the little girl's ear: the number ten is where Nani was violated. And the number fifteen. Once on the way up and once on the way back. And the number twelve. The fifty-five and the fifty-nine, too. But that was a month later. Did you hear what Nani said, sweets? Fifty-five, the girl sings softly. Mother's Little Helper raped Nani all those times. Different Mother's Little Helpers on different trolleybuses. But still one and the same. Did you hear what Nani said? The girl draws a skinny circle into the condensation of the window. For eyes she makes x's. The trolley sways here then there and its accordion-like midsection guffaws. There is a pervasive smell of sour cabbage and gasoline. The smell of suspicion. Mother's Little Helper is on this trolleybus, as well. The woman: next stop is ours, chicken. Have your mittens? Come. And they squeeze out of the bench seats and stagger up toward the door. The girl, passing through the accordion-like middle: ribs! They could be, sweets. We're like Pinocchio and Gepetto inside the whale. She is right, the wee one. The flexible midsection of the trolley has ribs. Better to support the pectoral girdle, you. Let's go you silly goat, the woman says. Pneumatic doors open. PneumaticPhlegmatic.

(ready mics, ready camera three . . . open their mics, take three)

There isn't much for a child to do in the park in winter, other than run around the lake or. Play with sticks. Stones. The woman buries her nose into her scarf. Wind cuts cold channels into the face. The child comes to her, brings her a handful of frozen pebbles from the shore of the lake and says: emeralds. Go play there, sweets. For a few minutes while Nani talks to a friend. All right. All right, chicken. There. Mother's Little Helper is here with them. Standing next to a frozen stone bench just to the side. He is dressed shabbily, hands in pockets, slimy hair, cheap brown scuffed shoes. When the woman comes to him he lights a cigarette. Hand trembles. What's the story, he says. Nothing. No story, he says. Nothing this week. He takes a small notepad and fountain pen from his breast and writes something. Hand trembles from the cutting wind. The woman looks back at the toddler. She squats by the edge of the lake and rearranges various rocks. Emeralds or. Bones. Mother's Little Helper: how old is she. Eighteen months about. *(ready two, take two)* What's that mean. I don't know, the woman says. What do you want it to mean. I mean is she talking yet. Mostly babbles, the woman now. Mother's Little Helper writes in his pad. What type of babbles. The usual. She's eighteen months. You said. I have it here, he says. Then, so. No story for this week? Nothing. All right, Mother's Little Helper says and shivers. From his breast pocket he removes a photograph. It is devoid of color. He hands it to her. She grips it but he holds for a second. Makes sure she sees. It is a photograph of her. Naked. Only from the breasts up. Compromised.

(ready one . . . take one)

Coming back to the child by the lake. Frozen. The toddler turns. Smiles. Stands. Runs to the woman. Chicken. Having fun, sweets? Having fun with your emeralds then. The child points: look. A white swan floats to them looking for bread or. Look. Swan lake. The bird floats. Floats. Inside, the woman feels hollow. The bird is menacing. And then. It stops swimming and leans to one side. Then the other. Something is wrong. Inside. The woman feels hollow watching this. The bird breaks into a circle. Over and over. First large then. The circles are tighter and tighter. Something inside the bird's brain is short-circuiting. Nothing works. The circles get tight enough until they can be made no more. It just rotates very quickly. And then the swan collapses on its side a few feet from them.

(ready two . . . take)
(ready three . . . take)
(open their mics)

The girl giggles and points to the swan now floating limply on half-frozen water. The head is beginning to sink, and the long neck is curved into an elegant L. Let's go chicken before we freeze here. Come on. As they exit the park the woman tears up the photograph and places the pieces into the rubbish bin. No use having the image. Mother has the negative.

(ready two . . . take two . . . close their mics . . . down to black, roll eleven, track eleven, up eleven)

CHEAP2
(Published in Flash Frontier, 2015)

one eighty-seven
for duckheads
seven of them chopped up
and staggered beak to brain
so they can fit tidily
in the Styrofoam tray
tightly wrapped in plastic
one eighty-seven
for duckheads
is nice and cheap
and will yield a week's worth of
head cheese
for a family

IN ANOTHER COUNTRY
(a shorter version of this appeared in The Miscreant, 2015)

HOLD ON, I'M COMING. Dig this.

First one checked in was my brother Petr. Was named after a saint. But he ended up among the stars after one year. I never knew him proper. I came just before he died. Of course, I never could know him proper. He had tuberculosis or some brain swelling, I don't remember now to tell. There've been a few. Two others came after me, a boy and a girl and both of them got thrown back up to the sky. Back to God. At least they were christened. The Church was there the first day, never mind both didn't yet have a name. The Church was always there the first day. For all of us. God delivers 'em dirty and wants 'em back clean. A fuck of a man He is, isn't he? And one more. There was one more when I turned four—a girl named

Violetta. She was run down by a taxi by mistake at the seaside on the 7th of July, 1975. And up to the stars she went with all the others. I remember not liking her too much. Babies are worthless, like I was. Healthy, rosy, tree trunks for legs, a strong chest and heartbeat, nine pounds and a half and worth less than a round piece of horse shite drying on pavement in the hot sun.

My Ma won't tell you that, but I could see it in her eyes as I punched through the air and squirmed to get to her tit. I don't remember St. Petr, but I remember that.

I came roaring in with a crooked nose in the middle of the day in the middle of the week in the middle of the summer. In another country. In a strange country.

"At's a good boy there," said the man who'd pulled my head with forceps as my Ma shoved me out with the innards an' all. Good riddance.

"At's a good strong boy."

"Gimme a cigarette," said my Ma. When they held me up for her to see she nodded and reclined back.

"Have to work on the boy's nose on your own, at home," said the man with the bloody forceps. "Should be no more than a few weeks if you do it daily. Cartilage, mum. She is a fickle material but fixable. The wonders of the human body, mum."

"Gimme a cigarette."

My Ma. By then she was already ruined. A big woman with no more dreams and four children in the stars.

My poor Ma.

She was called Lily. Lily. I think of the name and I don't see my mother. Lily is like a melody. Shiny, black hair, olive skin, a mole right there by the lip, in that little groove just below the nose. Bit to the right, off-center. She skips, she laughs, she plays hopscotch. Her arms dance with the wind, she is a fast learner. Her teacher is fond of her. She is good at maths and brilliant at calligraphy. She makes the cursive letters look like gems. She's a great future coming. She'll marry a big noise. Have healthy children. Live happily ever after. But what happens after? What of that? No one ever tells the story of ever after. The fairy tale always stops short.

My poor ruined mother.

She was twelve when she figured out her life would have no music. And she was nineteen when she plowed into my father—a Mack truck barreling through the air, eviscerating everything in his path with a heartbeat.

★

Mikey Beyer came off the parapet of rubbish and dirt, looking like a thick fuckin' idjit with that Legionnaire's hat stuffed down on top of his ears.

"I was jus' kiddin' yis, but lookit, at least you was payin' attention," he said and walked toward us, stupid grin on his face.

"Permission to clip him sir," Corey Boland said to the Captain.

"Denied. We can't spare the bullet."

"Hey, you fuckin' thick," yelled Patty Cassesse, "come up here and I'll peg you square in yer wooden forehead."

He pumped his BB gun and aimed.

"I was only havin' yous on," Mikey Beyer yelled.

Patty Cassesse pumped the rifle again and closed his left eye.

"It's the right one you close if yer left-handed Patty," said the Captain.

"Oh. Yeah."

"Lookit here," said Mikey Beyer now almost dead in front of us, the firing squad. "I was only havin' yous on, ye dumb Mick Wop."

Patty Cassesse dropped the BB rifle and made fists.

"Fuckin' Kraut, I'll kill ye . . ."

The Captain got in between the two of them and coddled the boys.

"Now shake you two. Shake on it."

They clasped hands and each squeezed as hard as he could. Then something hit Mikey Beyer and landed next to him. It was lit. It was one of our bottle rockets. Neely Murkowski had shot it from out of the bushes and pegged Mikey Beyer straight in the leg. It went off on the ground, and the three of them ducked.

"I was only havin' yous on," yelled Neely Murkowski coming out from behind the bush.

We roared.

The Captain stomped his boot into the dusty, pebbly road. "Fuckin' idjits, all a you. Jeesus . . . good for nothin' horseshits. Nobody ever listens to nobody. I'm goin' home."

Just then we saw Roxy come through with a burlap sack filled with new potatoes and a bottle of milk. All of us had it for Roxy. She was blonde with short hair, cut like those flapper girls from the 20s we saw in silent films at the Scalia cinema every Saturday. We didn't hardly ever see blonde girls in real life. The boys squeezed their lips together and made kissy-kissy sounds as she passed. She thrust her thumb in between her forefinger and middle finger, making a fist, and gave it out to all of us.

"Fuck yous all, yous hard-on gobshits."

And then all the boys laughed.

Roxy was something. She had an older sister, Andy, looked just like her but with jet black hair. The both of them swore like sailors. Fishwives is what Corey Boland called them. We was all in love with them at various times. But mostly throughout the summer, for some reason. Before Roxy took the corner and disappeared, she looked back and gave the Fuck You fist one more time.

We all laughed.

Because that's all we could do then. We were all of ten or twelve and looked like a band of homeless hooligans, most of us with wooden rifles or sticks and truncated branches, playing up Army soldiers.

"Fuckin' gypsies," someone yelled down to us from a balcony. "Go home to your mammies and study math."

We looked but we couldn't see the coward. He'd ducked back into his flat.

"Surrender now, ye fuckin' waster," Charley Swatters offered up, and launched a nasty gob of spit up toward the insult. We all ducked when the phlegmy mass came down.

"Jeeeesus."

"Charley, you thick fuck. Dontcha know anything about gravity?"

And we roared. All of us. You could hear it around corners. You could hear it over the sounds of people beating the dust out of their rugs.

★

Three of them were beating the horse with branches the size of small tree trunks. The other one, the man with the crumpled fedora, stood in the courtyard sharpening something that looked like a machete. The peasants had been drinking and playing backgammon. Something must have happened in the middle of their games. The playing boards were open on the large outdoor table and wooden pieces were strewn about carelessly on and off their respective triangles. Small glasses of red wine were left suddenly and unfinished. Ugly black flies were circling, sometimes landing and probing the drying juice on the rims. The animal was down and foaming at the mouth from the effort to live. The men were relentless. The blows came to the head two by two, but the animal refused to die. One of them was swinging at the legs and the spine. We could hear the bones snap from across the road.

"It takes two men *and* my Da to bring down the pig at Christmas," Cesar said and spat into the dusty road.

I did the same. I don't know why. Probably because it made me look tough watching the bloody scene.

"Let's go," he said. "We can steal some boysenberries from the mayor's tree up the road there."

"He's got hounds loose in the yard."

"They's branches hanging down over the fence and into the road. Fair game. I can hoist you on my back so's you can pick 'em. Or you can hoist me. I don't care."

"I don't care either."

He took out a wrinkled cigarette from his pocket.

"Whaddya think they're gonna do with the horse," I said.

"I don't know. Stew, probably."

"Yea. They's gonna have to give the fair share to the State, though."

"Yea."

"Here." He gave me the cigarette. "Pavel rolled it," he said. "It's not that Marasesti shit you buy at the cooperative."

"All right."

"You can chew mint afterwards if you're scared they'll smell it on your breath. It's all over the fields. If you're worried."

"All right."

"Don't worry."

"I'm not.

And I spat into the dust and held my hands in my pockets like I'd seen Bogart do in the movies.

★

"What're you seeing through there?"

The boy held his face close to the fence. His right eye covered the hole's entire circumference. He pushed his forehead into the mildewy slat to cut out most of the extraneous light sneaking in between flesh and wood.

"Carny? Can you hear me sweetie? What's it look like?"

"What're you askin' him for, he's a fuckin' retard."

"Shut it, he's not retarded."

The boy pushed in his head as hard as he could, hoping to cut out all sound, as well. The fence gave a little to the perpendicular pressure. The wood cracked from the distress.

"Look it, he's gonna break the fuckin' fence. I'm telling you."

"Shut it. You don't know anything."

"I know he's a retard. Yous all a bunch of retards. Your fuckin' family like."

"Shut it."

★

"Carny? What's it look like sweetie?"

"What're you askin' a retard for?"

CORNETE

IN JANUARY 1980, we were stuck in the cracks between the politics of three countries, waiting for paperwork to clear us from the East into the West and then across the ocean to Cleveland, Ohio to start a new, better life.

We idled in Rome at the Pensione La Scala, a rooming house across from a porno theatre and an *osteria*, which sold head cheese by the slice with mustard in a container on the side. Our room was small: two single beds, one sink and mirror, no hot water. We washed our hands and feet in the small basin twice a day. We brushed our teeth at night with paste that smelled of sulfur and tasted worse.

The toilet was down the hall and shared with a floor of chain smokers who left their shoes on the doormat, outside their rooms, and held their lit cigarettes out the cracked door into the hallway of the rooming house. Looking down, the scene was surreal: human arm segments holding smoking ciggies, casual chatter coming from behind the doors. The shower worked on coins, like a pay phone. You had to constantly feed it while you were under the water. Hot water was more expensive.

For three weeks, we waited for our paperwork to be processed at the American Embassy. We waited for the American Dream—Cleveland.

During the day, my father would walk everywhere to see the ruins. He even walked to another country one day—the Vatican. And then the next he walked there again. I went with him that time into the Sistine Chapel and saw the Pieta enclosed in a box of glass. But mostly, while he walked the city, I stayed in the room and made *cornete* out of sheets of paper—smoothly shaped, stealthy, rolled-up spiral projectiles, which I launched from a long, plastic segment of thin pipe by blowing hard. I shot them out of our fifth-floor window at parked cars. I didn't have the courage to launch them at people. I was afraid of Italians. I was afraid of them reaching up five floors. I was afraid of most people then. Now I simply just don't like them.

I once set off a car alarm with one of these *cornete*. The *Carabinieri* came after almost an hour and towed the screaming Fiat down the long street, toward The Colosseum, to the applause of a crowd gathered.

There were other foreigners stuck in this weird, interim freedom camp just like us, some of them waiting perpetually for their entry visas into the United States. Albanians, Bulgarians, Yugoslavians. The entire *pensione* was full of émigrés idling. Some of them had been there for over a year with no end to their internment in sight.

A decrepit, Russian man gave me a small, metal memento of Mishka The Bear, the mascot of the Moscow Summer Olympics. Carter had announced America was boycotting the Games that year. Something to do with Afghanistan and the Soviets. I was ten so I didn't care that much for politics, even though we were caught up in them. All of us were.

The old Russian carried with him a little notebook with phrases translated into English: "Yes, I would like a drink please." "Pardon, do you know where the nearest bar is?" "Felicitations on your engagement, I would very much prefer to share a drink with you." "Would you like a drink?" "This is grounds for a celebration; let's have a drink." "An egg in an egg cup." "Dick is in bed." "This is the house that Jack built."

None of it made any sense. But I did what I was told. I went where I was told something really good was waiting.

The Russian hoped to get to California. He had no one out there. He must have been seventy. Sometimes, in between the meals served at the *pensione*, he would help me roll *cornete* for my plastic tube. He had leather, peasant hands and he constructed the best paper projectiles I'd ever seen. They flew with the precision of missiles. My father, who spoke a little Russian and talked with the old man from time to time, said he had been in the Red Army during the war. He had loaded shells into the 152-mm M1937 howitzer guns that fought back the Germans.

Our visas came through on January 25th. On our last day in Rome, my father and I went down the hall to the shower with a fistful of *lira* and fed them into the slot while we worked quickly and washed our hair with hot water. We wanted to be clean and look fresh for Cleveland, Ohio.

THE DECADENCE OF WESTERN CULTURE: RALEIGH, NORTH CAROLINA OR MOLES LOVE CANDY

WALTER HEIBESEN WAS ONLY ever at ease when pulling weeds from his flowerbeds. He wasn't much of a gardener or an outdoor type in general—in fact he'd despised camping ever since he was eight years of age and had fallen into a near full outhouse at a camping ground in Missoula, Montana during summer holidays with his uncle—but Walter felt a strange, unexplored connection to the earth and an enormous, almost spiritual satisfaction pulling invasive plants from his property. The meaner and nastier the weed was, the happier it made

Walter. But not for the obvious reason. Upon pulling out the plant, he would inspect its roots and marvel at the intricacies of the system, and at the speed with which the plant grew its subterranean tuber. He respected the choking weeds and their vigorous desire to live and propagate even within the smallest spaces in between boulders in the most arid of climates. He talked to them, cajoled them, and sometimes even apologized for removing them from their nutrient-rich home.

Walter loved crabgrass invasions the most. After removal they left deep holes in the turf, which of course satisfied Walter, but which neighbors mistook for mole tunnels, thus sending unnecessary tremors and panic throughout the neighborhood association of cross-property-infestation. "Use chocolate or candy," was among the stranger, unsolicited opinions Walter received one day from a heavy-set, over-painted Southern belle. "Moles love candy. Especially cotton candy." The thought of baiting nonexistent underground pests with fluffy, pink, spun sugar made Walter smile inside. Absurdity and futility together made for a colorful existence. And at that moment, Walter stopped hearing the woman who spent her days across the street at 229 Parklands Lane, planning out her daughter's debutante party at an oversized dining table in front of a gargantuan bay window with the curtains always open, so everyone could see that she was busy with important work. At that moment, Walter felt happy.

One Saturday afternoon, Walter found a Baby Ruth carefully laid out as bait at the mouth of a deeper hole left by the removal of a *Digitaria spp*. He left it there for a colony of ants to enjoy.

Pulling crabgrass by hand was Walter Heibesen's Big Two-Hearted River, even though he'd never read anything by Hemingway. But Walter knew that squatting and kneeling and sweating drops of salty fluid from eccrine and apocrine glands down into the earth was healing him faster than any chemicals he'd been advised to take twice a day with an eight-ounce glass of water and on a full stomach by his ex-wife's psychiatrist.

Twice a year—usually in April and September—he would inadvertently douse himself with poison ivy oils, the source of which he never found, although Walter didn't really know what poison ivy or poison oak looked like (so it could have been any of the plants he pulled with his bare hands). Nor was he interested in finding out. The skin irritation he suffered every season became a ritual and, at the risk of believing and labeling himself a sadist, he enjoyed the hardship that nature offered. It went with working the land. It went with healing himself.

As Walter Heibesen became increasingly ill during the summer of his fifty-second year, the neighborhood association passed covenants that mandated the use of a specific lawn service company, which would heavily discount its strange-smelling products to homeowner members. Now, mostly living inside, Walter developed paralyzing migraine headaches, which left him with severe vertigo and hunger. At the end of November, he lost sight in his right eye and could no longer formulate any words, although his thinking was clear and logical. Illness was in his cells. But illness had always been all around.

When the moving truck pulled out its side ramp and bridged the gap between the cold, winter asphalt and the hibernating fescue turf of what was once Walter Heibesen's home, the Southern belle was sat at the dining table in front of the Cyclopean bay window (as usual), drapes pulled to the side so everyone could see that the winter cotillion she was planning for a select four couples—one of whom was her daughter and her new beau—was the most important event that year, short of the neighborhood association Christmas party, which was to take place at the Deerborne Country Club and was to feature a jazz legend diva who was being flown in on everyone's dime from Williamsburg, New York.

The woman, having stopped writing with her ball point pen, craned her neck just slightly to try to get a look at the new owners of Walter's house. But all she saw were the moving men and their crystallizing breath as they panted and lifted pieces of maple and cherry furniture wrapped in dark green blankets. Then, suddenly, she puffed out a quick burst of air in hope that the new owners would comply with the covenants and treat their property in the spring with the appropriate, strange-smelling chemicals that were to be supplied at a discount by the TruChem Lawn Care Company.

THE DECADENCE OF WESTERN CULTURE: HOLLYWOOD OR MAKING CONVERSATION IN A BAR MAKING SOAP INTO A BAR

NOW HERE'S HOW you do it.

For every four fingers of good whiskey you down a glass of water. At the beginning, you pop a couple of B12 vee-tamins. Good for the liver. Balances levels of CDT, MCV, and hepatic enzymes GGT. To temper the maelstrom that is to come later in the night, ingest a couple of cups of strong java intermittently.

What I loathe the most is being served drinks by bartenders with baseball hats on backwards.

I once ordered Johnnie Walker "neat" and got back a pint glass full of ice and water, with a bit of whiskey floating around. It looked like iced tea. Served by an Asian frat boy type with a dirty baseball cap. On backwards.

Dolt.

"You hear about the man with maggots in his eyes who died?"

"No."

"They found him in a nursing home in Deltona, Florida. Man had maggots in one of his eyes, an infected breathing tube, a partially inserted catheter, and bed sores. Apparently he was under constant care."

"Sounds like he was."

Now here's how you do it.

For every liter-and-a-half bottle of red wine, you crank out a multi-veetamin and a cup of espresso with anisette. No more than three smokes per night. And frequent trips to the washroom to process out the sulfites.

"That 94-year-old man they found in Morristown, Tennessee had his hand cut off."

"Did he now?"

"They're thinking it was some kind of botched robbery."

"Do they now?"

"Found a couple of butcher knives right next to the body. They're saying he died a horrible death."

"We all do."

"Do we now?"

Now here's how you do it. Put on your gloves and goggles. Be careful with the lye. Read the label. It is a caustic and dangerous substance. It makes wonderful soap, but it is not your friend. It'll burn a hole in your skin. The first thing you need to do is put your scale in your sink, place the empty container on it, THEN turn on the scale, THEN start pouring your water in. Weigh 32 ounces of COLD water in a plastic container. Never use hot water to mix with lye, it will volcano! Very slowly, pour the lye into the cold water. Make sure you leave everything in the sink. It is safer that way. Lye has a lot of static cling, so spills are easy to do. You'll notice the lye reacts with the cold water and it gets very hot. It'll also give off a gas, that's why you should be outside. Don't breathe the fumes. When it is stirred, put the cap on the lye solution and bring it back inside. Let your lye sit in a safe place until it cools off to room temperature. This will take two to three hours. When the lye gets back down to room temperature, you're ready to start making your soap. Start weighing out your fats. Put the pot full of fats on the stove. Heat on the stove, stirring often. Keep a close eye on it because it reaches temperature somewhat quickly. Stir well before taking its temperature. You're looking for something between 120 and 130 degrees Fahrenheit. When your fats reach that, put your pot in the sink. If you made the lye solution the day before, it is now at room temperature. Put on your gloves and goggles. Very carefully and slowly pour the lye solution into the fats. Use a large spoon to stir it in. Hold your head back while pouring to avoid any splash back getting you. Once the lye solution is mixed in, use the stick blender. Use it off and on. Careful, continuous use will blow it up. Blend for a minute, stir with a spoon for a minute, that kind of thing. You should come to a very thick soap with this equipment, probably in about five minutes. You will see changes in your creation. It will immediately start to become more opaque. It will become thicker and more opaque as time goes on. This is the mixture changing into soap. Immediately pour your soap into your molds. Let it sit undisturbed in a warm room for 24 hours. As the chemical reaction is taking place it generates heat. If you put your hand on the side of the box in about 1 hour, you will feel its warmth. That's it. Oh yea, grab some pH testing papers. The soap ought to fall in the 7–9 category.

THE DECADENCE OF WESTERN CULTURE: TUCUMCARI, NEW MEXICO, 1990 (A SNAPSHOT)
(Published in Maudlin House, 2015)

"JUDAS CHRIST, this all looks like the Coyote and Roadrunner cartoons," Val said. "This is some kind of surreal moonscape or . . . what the hell is this."

"You ever seen dried-up lava fields? The breeze whistles The Funeral March 'round four every afternoon. And Pele comes like a siren from within and makes sausages for all the wide-eyed tourists."

"Christ. Funeral March. Who the hell is that."

"Chopin."

"All right. I'll see you that and raise you a walk on the circumference of the meteor crater in Arizona."

We had been through the worst storm of our lives. The crosswinds shook us all the way from Amarillo into Tucumcari. The hail was, at times, baseball-sized. Later, in the motel, we watched on the telly gusts hit up to 85 and footage of a poor sap sporting a mullet in an orange Karmann Ghia close to Palomas who had been blown over and violated by the elements. We ate mealy letters made from gelatinous pasta straight out of cans and flipped through the local channels: college b-ball, The Clapper, I've fallen and I can't get up. We smoked in the bathroom with the fan on. Then later. In the tub. Each one of us separately. Our personal time alone with a can of Olympia beer: *It's the Water!*

(No, it's the economy, stupid!)

"There's nothing here."

"People live here."

"Where. In the ground?"

I put gas in the tank and Val lit up right at the pump.

"You're gonna kill us."

"We should maybe send a postcard," he said.

"You're right . . . I feel like we're in a John Ford movie."

"Missing you, wish you were here . . . or . . . wish you were missing . . ."

"Tumbleweeds would make it perfect."

Val laughed. And spat into the dust. His coagulated saliva made a little wet crater. He kicked up brown earth and covered it up in a weird gesture of respect.

I bought a handful of arrowheads and two Kachina dolls from an Indian stand next to the gas pumps. The man selling was very old and had a dusty cowboy hat. I hated cowboy hats. I hated cowboys.

"Fuckin' Indians," Val said, "they despise us."

"They're right."

"Why. We're not even from this country."

"That's why."

THE DECADENCE OF WESTERN CULTURE: GREENBELT, MARYLAND OR BUD'S WAREHOUSE

KEVIN THE JOCK drives us in every morning. A shitty AMC Eagle that smells like patchouli inside. Before we pull up to the dock, we smoke in the car with the windows cracked down half an inch. It's our three minutes of peace before we start unloading semis full of boxed food from Richmond, Virginia. Richfood. Most of the time the trailers aren't air-conditioned, so we need to work fast unloading, then stocking and distributing the supplies on the shelves inside. The boss is Ted. Ted is an overweight but diminutive man with remnants of hair and a mustache. He's a lifer. He wears polyester slacks and collared shirts with short sleeves. Physically he is Andy Sipowicz incarnate, only we don't know about Andy Sipowicz yet. Kevin and I are students working our summers through community college. Well . . . I am, Kevin plays a sport that will yield him millions if he's lucky and doesn't become injured. But he will. He'll blow out the ACL. Really, we're all lifers somewhere even if it's just putting in time at the machines temporarily. Kevin will be a lifer at a chicken slaughterhouse on the outskirts of Los Angeles. He'll work the night shift and he'll get to park on a vacant lot full of gravel out back from a Chinese food place that also cashes checks and serves Philly cheesesteaks.

★

Hey, that's it, Ted says coming through the double doors, as we walk up to the dock. That's it. He says that and makes a slashing motion on his neck, then whistles. That's that. And then sips from a small, Styrofoam cup of coffee.

I'm sorry fellas.

Greta too?

Yea, Ted says. I called her last night.

And Kevin and I walk back to the smoky Eagle.

What do you wanna do?

We should go somewhere. Get a drink.

I mean what should we do. About jobs. Besides, no one serves this early.

I don't know. Don't you have a rich uncle or something?

Kevin laughs through his nose and makes a small bubble of mucus.

Things work out right, I get a tryout for the Hoyas, Kevin says.

Yea. Gotta quit smoking herb though. They test your piss now.

I'll use your piss.

That's even worse. They'll have you in prison.

Yea, Kevin laughs. What should we do?

I don't know. But I'll miss the Little Debbie's man on Fridays.

The vendor guy?

Yea.

And after a long time standing beside the car he says: Fuck this city.

And after a long time again he says: I just need to make it to September. To my tryout with the Hoyas.

Yea.

We should go somewhere, though.

Yea. But no one serves this early.

Yea. I know, Kevin says. Goddamn motherfucking city. Capital of the motherfucking world.

MOVING THROUGH
(Published in the Romanian literary journal EgoPHobia, 2013)

I DREAMED OF GEPETTO and his impossible puppets with their growing body parts, carved out of stray logs found by neighbors. The strings to one of his marionettes had become tangled, and the wooden creature was suspended in an unstable, weird, macabre pose with one leg wrapped around his neck waiting for rescue.

"Hang him from the handle of the stove and let him dry there. And then come on. There's mint tea."

The old man brought sliced, fried eggplant and we both sat down and drank olive oil from small thimbles. The thick liquid was spicy and cut into the tongue capriciously. He threw a pinch of coarse sea salt over his shoulder. And then another onto his plate.

"Did you know Pinocchio is Tuscan for pine nut?"

"My daughter likes fairies."

The siren across the river signaled the end of third shift at the factory. He pushed a wooden cutting block toward my plate. He had sliced fat pieces of ham and arranged them like a deck of cards fanning out.

"Which one is her favorite?"

"The Turquoise Fairy."

"Tonight, at bedtime, tell her the story of the magic flower swing."

We played backgammon in the afternoon and he used brill cream in his hair to smooth it down and keep it from lifting in the wind. He rolled the bones after blowing for luck into his fist and pushed his wooden men around the board.

"You are not moving through wisely," he said.

He slid his men counterclockwise and bumped me onto the bar.

"You see?" he said.

"It's impossible on this board. It's clogged up. You've clogged up all the points."

The siren across the river signaled the end of first shift at the factory. He went to the back room to bring out paper money. The currency was out of season. He gave me a small metal key to a weathered valise that was waiting by the front door. On the walls, there were pictures of a badly drawn boy and Cyrillic writing in black ink.

"The man who did those died in a horrible skiing accident. He was a communist."

He pointed with his head to a daguerreotype of a funeral. It was framed and hanging on the wall, in the kitchen, by the adobe hearth.

"Tell your little girl if she keeps jumping on the bed, I'll hide pins and needles inside the mattress. Tell her that."

THE GIRL WHO LOVED TO STRIKE MATCHES (A FAIRY TALE)
(Published in The Airgonaut, 2016)

"WHAT HAPPENED?"

She looked down at her bare feet. The snowflakes clung to her long hair. It looked like they were slowly arranging themselves into a white hat for her. She was tiny and seemed like she was floating inside an oversized, cut-out burlap sack.

"What happened? Where are your shoes?"

"They were slippers," she said. "And they were too big. They were my mum's, besides."

"Well, what happened to them? It's frigid."

"They fell off. I lost them crossing the street. One of them. The other was taken away by a boy who wanted to make a cradle out of it, for when he would have children."

"I know that."

"It's a good story, isn't it," she said.

"It is. I read it when I was seven years old."

She snickered and rubbed one blue frozen foot with the other.

"I read you and Jules Verne and Renart the Fox."

"Which did you like the most," she said.

"Jules Verne."

"Which Jules Verne?"

"Twenty thousand leagues under the sea."

"Naturally. You were a boy. All boys love a good sea adventure."

"From that I learned the word *maelstrom*."

"Well, what is it?"

"It's like letting the water out of your bathtub. The big swirl as it goes down the drain. That's what it is."

She snickered and blew warm air into her hands.

"Where are your matches? You're supposed to have a bundle. You're supposed to keep warm by striking them against the frozen walls of the houses."

"I sold them," she said.

"That's not how the story goes."

"I know. But the end is the same."

"Why? Aren't you bringing home money?"

"No. I gave it away to the pauper with the fiddle."

"All of it?"

"It was just matches," she said. "It wasn't that much money."

"Who will find you in the morning?"

"The townspeople."

"The end *is* the same."

"I told you. The end is always the same," she said.

"I didn't like your story because of God."

"Why God."

"I didn't believe in him."

"Not even when you were a boy," she said.

"No."

"What did you believe in then?"

"Once, at Easter, my father made giant rabbit footprints out of flour. I believed that."

"And then you lived happily ever after?"

"I don't know. I don't think so."

She giggled and shifted her weight and shivered.

"Where will you be? I'll call out to them, the townspeople."

She pointed to an alley in between two homes.

"Wait some time before you summon them," she said. "They are not supposed to find me until I'm frozen. It's how the story ends."

She giggled and walked away, barefoot, on the ice. She turned into the alley and squatted down and pulled her feet under her burlap sack. Then she shifted on her side, facing the cold concrete wall.

"All right."

Once upon a time . . .